ISBN-13: 9798613249169
ISBN-10: 1477123456

Cover design by: Art Painter
Library of Congress Control Number: 2018675309
Printed in the United States of America

PREFACE

A few definitions of the word *devil*

an atrociously wicked, cruel, or ill-tempered person
or
a person, usually one in unfortunate or pitiable circumstances
or
a person who is very clever, energetic, reckless, or mischievous

and so on and so on.........

THE DEVIL'S IN THE DETAILS

an Abby Lynn Novella Book 4

www.lyndafreeman.com

Chapter 1

The ER doctor finished his examination and told Abby that Colin's condition was not severe but critical. Reassuring her that the induced coma was a precaution. So that he and the bullet would not move. The doctor said, "he would pull through this and fully recover once we remove the bullet."

The surgery was the next day. Abby was beside herself with worry. She thanked Joe and Marty for staying with her but encouraged them to go home and get some rest. Abby said she would call them with any updates. Jim was also gone, and he said he would return later.

Amanda and Rachel were on their way to the hospital with a change of clothes and some food for Abby. Rachel commented to Amanda as to why she was so upset. She confessed to her sister that she truly loved Colin like a father. Rachel just rolled her eyes in disbelief upon hearing this news. Amanda asked Rachel, "why anyone would shoot Colin?" Rachel exhibited no concern at all for Colin, let alone their mom.

Amanda called Colin's daughter Maddie with the news that her father had been shot and was having surgery tomorrow. Amanda did mention that they expected him to make a full recovery. Rachel reminded Amanda that Maddie was pregnant. Rachel thought telling her was wrong, considering Maddie was almost ready to deliver. She deserves to know Rach what if something horrible happens to Colin; he's her dad.

Alone in the hospital waiting room, Abby found the most comfortable chair she could find and settled down. She got out her note pad and started making notes regarding the events of the last few weeks. Her goal was to follow the leads, but she needed Colin's phone, and it was locked as always, so Abby tried to unlock it but to no avail. Well shit!

Abby needed to call Auggie and leave it up to him to tell others about Colin or not to tell. More than likely, Jim had already tried to contact him. What is the protocol for a time like this? Again Abby finds herself with no answers. Auggie would have the answers to some of her questions; Abby was sure of that.

Almost asleep Abby's phone rings, what the hell it's after midnight. Blake, no way I'm answering his call!

Blake was disappointed Abby did not answer; he knew where she was. Rachel told him. Would he be pleased if her husband didn't make it? Hell yes, he would, but Blake doubted it would make a difference in their relationship. He decided to text, "Abby, I heard about your husband, and I just wanted to say how sorry I am and hope he has a full recovery, love Blake."

As Abby read the text, she was appalled. No way in hell he cared what happened to Colin! Unfortunately, Abby suspected that the only way Blake knew was because Rachel told him. I need to set my daughter straight about many things, especially being loyal to her family. I swear I will cut her off if she does not change her attitude.

Fuming mad and overly stressed, Abby decided to take one of the "relaxing" pills the doctor gave her. Not long after taking the medication, she was sleeping, setting her alarm for six a.m. in the morning.

When Abby woke up, she saw that the girls did indeed bring her change of clothes and some food for breakfast. They left a note and said they would be back in the morning. Abby found a restroom and changed her clothes and freshened up. She headed for the cafeteria for some breakfast and coffee. She saw Jim and Joe in the cafeteria having coffee. Upon seeing them, she says, "well, this is a site I never thought I'd see again." Abby, any updates for Colin, the two of them, said in unison. No, not yet, I called the floor, and they said they were preparing him for surgery. I'm going to the waiting room now, wanna come along? I could use the company.

Maxim was pleased with himself, yes, very pleased indeed.

Going out was what he needed not only to foil his boredom, but he did get some interesting intel. His instincts were spot on with thinking he would run into some bad dudes in that bar. Rumor has it that The Snowman has been, should we say "sidelined" by a bullet. Of course, no info on who or why? Could this be what Nikolai was referring too? Why would he know about this hit? Did he do it? If so, why? Too many unanswered questions.

Joe, Jim, and the girls waited with Abby in the surgical waiting room. She was allowed to see Colin before they wheeled him off. He was, of course, sleeping or still in a coma. Abby kissed her husband on the forehead and whispered in his ear, "I promise I will find out who did this to you, I owe you that, I love you pops." Little did she know was that Colin could hear her but was unable to respond.

When Abby came out of the room, Amanda and Rachel both hugged her. "Thanks, girls, for coming." Geez, mom, we would never leave you here by yourself. I know girls, and I appreciate it none the less. Waiting and waiting got on all of their frayed nerves. Jim was always on his cell texting. Joe drank so much coffee that we thought he would explode from a caffeine high. Small talk didn't exist among the group; what did any of them have in common, nothing would come to mind. Rachel had her earbuds in listening to music. Amanda was reading on her kindle app, and Abby was praying to herself.

It was like something out of a movie, a handsome doctor with white surgical garb on comes out of a set of double doors, pulling off his mask. He holds up his hand to signal us that he had news. Abby's knees wobbled as she tried to get up. Joe noticed and caught her just in time; he was sure she was going to faint. The four of them circled the surgeon and waited with bated breath for whatever news he had.

Mrs. Cavanaugh, the surgery went well; we removed the bullet without any further damage. *Relief!* The other wounds will heal with time, but the spinal injury will take time and require additional treatments. Your husband will not be going any-where for some time due to needing extensive rehabilitation. If he wasn't in such excellent physical condition, this might have turned out differently. Abby thanked the doctor and asked when he would be awake. Give it about an hour, or so then you and only you can see him.

Everyone hugged and cried with the news. Even though Colin had a lengthy recovery period, it sounded like he would recover completely. Damn it, though, Abby, I should have asked how long a long recovery is? I need to keep notes, so I don't forget to ask the right questions.

Joe and Jim left to go back to the office. The girls and Abby went to get something to eat, and Amanda wanted to know if Abby wanted them to stay. No, you girls go back to school, and when I see him, I will call with an update. Oh, and please, Amanda, would you call Maddie and let her know how it went? Of course, mom, talk later then.

Again Abby found herself in an uncomfortable chair in the wait-ing room by herself. She continued to make notes and plans. With an hour to kill, she decided to call Maxim if anyone knew he would, or so she thought.

Maxim was recovering from a horrible headache caused by too much vodka last night. Oh shit that ringer is killing my head, he reached for the phone and saw the call was from Abby. Interest-ing that she didn't use our secret code. Maxim was sure he knew why she was calling and expected her to do so, but this was sooner than he thought.

Abby, I'm pleased to hear from you. How are you doing, my dear? Maxim, this is not a social call. I know that Abby, what can I do for you? So, I was right; you do know what happened to Colin? I do Abby, and before you ask, I had nothing to do with it. Oh my god, that never even entered my mind, Maxim, why would you think I would? That should be obvious, Abby; he has you I want you. But I am an honorable man I would not kill to have any woman, even you.

That was a lie because he would kill to have her!

Maxim, I need your help; I want to find out who shot my husband. What makes you think I can help? Are you serious, do you people think I'm an idiot, some dumb housewife or what? Abby, "no one thinks you are stupid or anything of the kind." Maxim, I do, of course, think you can help. Isn't this what you do for a living Maxim?

No, my dear, I do not investigate shootings; I am usually the "shooter" Abby. So are you going to help me or what? Let me think about this, Abby, let me gather any information I can, and I will get back to you. Abby, how is he doing? Colin is a survivor, and he will make a full recovery, thanks for asking. I may not like that The Snowman is married to you, Abby, but I do have professional respect for the man.

I needed to wait for Maxim to get back to me. In the meantime, going against my better judgment, I needed to get Jim involved, but of course, he more than likely already was. Abby expected Jim to visit Colin any time now then I will speak to him about the darker side of their business. I can suck up with the best of them if need be, and Jim will never know what hit him.

Abby was waiting in the surgical waiting room when Jim walked in. Hi Abby, any updates on Colin? No, not yet, they expect to wake him from the coma any time now. Jim, can I talk to you for a moment about something? Of course, Abby, what's on your mind? I have been going over mine and Colin's movements for the last week or so and have jotted down all I can remember. And you are doing this for what purpose Abby? Jim, I want to know why Colin was a target and who did it? Abby dear, people are working on this investigation as we speak; surely you know the bureau is involved. And his own company is investigating as well. I think Joe could provide information on Centry's case. Thanks, Jim, but I think I'm going to do what I can myself. Abby, you are treading on dangerous ground. No time like the present to get involved in my husband's business, Jim. Colin won't like this one-bit Abby, so my advice is to leave the investigating to the professionals. Yea, you're probably right, thanks for the information.

No way in hell I'm backing off from this I owe Colin for all he has done for me.

Chapter 2

Rachel needed a break from the events happening in their lives and, in particular, her sister. Amanda was on her last nerve, Colin, this and Colin that. Big sister was making her want to vomit because of her never-ending adoration for the man.

Rachel walked into the Mall Bar even though she was not twenty-one, yet she certainly looked it. Having a fake ID helps, and no one here knows she is Abby's daughter. She was not in the least worried about being seen.

Blake arrived a few minutes later. Rachel flagged him to her table. "Rachel, it's good to see you." He hugged her and sat down, he ordered a beer and asked Rachel how she managed to get hers? Has it been that long since college Blake? Ouch, and yes, it has been quite a while. Fake ID Blake, that's how you get in!

So. How's your stepfather doing? Yuck, he is nothing to me, and unfortunately, I hear he will eventually make a full recovery. Wow, Rachel, tell me how you really feel! I just did, and I have no love for the man, I leave that to my sister. Dang, you hate Colin that much? Hell yes I do, that man is not what mom thinks him to be. Well, I don't agree with you on that point. I believe Abby knows her husband exceptionally well.

So, Rachel, is there something specific you wanted to discuss? Yes, your favorite subject, my mother. Rachel, to be clear, I am not the kiss and tell kind of guy, especially to you. So, Blake, you agree then that you have kissed my mom? Oh, for god's sake, that was just a figure of speech, and you know it. Whatever you say, Blake, but I know you and mom have been doing the deed for many years. And Rach, you are basing that on what exactly?

Mom's journals!

Blake's face was so pale Rachel thought he might pass out. Earth to Blake, are you okay? Far from it, Rachel, are you saying Abby kept journals with personal and intimate information? Yes, and they were filled with quite the juicy stories indeed. Oh my god, have you told anyone else about those journals? Nobody else would care, except maybe Colin. Rachel noticed Blake's look was not of surprise but of knowing. *Blake, you know what's written, don't you?* That is pure speculation on your part. No, it is not, and you are so busted, Blake.

Rachel this is very important, how long has it been since you read those journals? Why do you want to know that? Please, young lady, answer the question? Oh, for god's sake, Blake, it has been a while. How long Rachel weeks, months? Okay, it was long before she met Colin, so last summer.

Blake felt some relief, but not entirely, Abby's journals were very shall we say "vivid" in nature. Her kids had no business reading their mother's personal diaries. Embarrassed, Blake was blushing severely. Blake, "when I found the journals, I never expected to read such intimate details of my mom's love life." But I am not a child any longer in case you haven't noticed. Anyway, when mom and Colin went out of town, I looked for more journals and found none; they were all gone.

Rach, you know Abby and I have been together on and off for my years. Of course, I know that. And I am sure you know we were having an affair when she was still married to your dad. Yes, both Amanda and I knew because she told us. Good grief is anything sacred?

It's crucial, Rachel, that you know Abby and I have not been together for many months. Of course, we had to see each other recently due to the trial, but that's been over for weeks now. Unfortunately for me, your mother is very much in love with her husband. A guy knows when it's time to give up and move on. That's precisely what I intend to do, give up. Blake, I don't believe you, I'm sorry, but I don't think you have given up. I think mom is still enamored with Colin, and eventually, that will diminish in time. I believe and always will that she loves you and will end up with you.

Wishful thinking, but I can't see that fairy tale happening. Rachel, please promise me you have not told anyone about the journals. Just you, Blake. Promise me you will never divulge what's in those journals to anyone; it would be very humiliating to me if you did. God, I promise I will not tell anyone about them. I wouldn't do anything to hurt you, Blake. If moving forward without mom is what you want, I certainly couldn't blame you for doing so. Thank you, Rachel. Let's eat. I'm starving.

Blake could not wait to leave because inside he was worried sick. If Rachel ever told anyone, let alone Colin, he knew he was doomed. Possibly since Rachel thinks Abby and I have not seen each other for months, she may not be tempted to gossip. Thank God she didn't see any entries in recent months. Hopefully, Abby has destroyed all of those damn journals.

Rachel thought about her and Blakes' luncheon and decided that she did not in the remotest sense believe he and Abby did not see each other. He was way too worried to be believable. Man, I wish I would have made copies of those journals.

Abby was still sitting close to Colin, waiting for him to wake up. His nurse said, "every patient is affected differently to anesthesia." He'll be coming around any time now. Regardless the waiting was hell. She left the room to use the restroom and stopped to let the guys know that he was not awake yet and would let them know when he was.

When Abby returned to the room, she saw the nurse hovering over him, taking his vitals. The nurse pointed toward Colin's eyes. Movement and action were starting. That's when Abby saw his eyes were undeniably opening. Abby quickly moved to his bedside just in time to barely hear him say, "darling, I'm okay and so sorry to worry you." Pops, who said I was worried, but anytime you want to stay out of the way of stray bullets, I wouldn't mind," Colin replies, "Abby Lynn, that goes double for you, now we're even."

Abby leaned in and kissed her guy on the forehead. Colin reached for her hand and squeezed it gently, holding onto it until he fell asleep. She left the room and told the guys he did wake up, but only for a few minutes then fell asleep again. Abby then suggested maybe they should leave and return tomorrow. Joe and Jim both agreed they would wait for her text to let them know when to visit. Joe hugged Abby and suggested she get some sleep; after all, she just got over her health issues.

Rachel found Abby in the waiting room on the ICU floor. Mom, mom wake up. Oh, Rachel, I must have fallen asleep. Mom, have you eaten dinner? No, Rach, I haven't would you like to go with me to the cafeteria for some much-needed food. Of course, I'll go, mom. I want you to take care of yourself. Thanks, Rachel, by the way, have you heard from Amanda? No, not since seeing her here yesterday. Mom, has Colin woke up yet? He did but for a short time, and then he was fast asleep again.

After eating dinner, Abby suggested Rachel go on home because she didn't think anyone could visit Colin in the ICU. Rachel left not long after dinner and with no regrets for not being able to see Colin. Abby caught off guard with Rachel's visit. Abby knew full well how she felt about him. But it was a nice gesture, none the same.

Chapter 3

Maxim sent a coded and encrypted message to Nikolai. Could helping Abby find the culprit who shot her husband get my foot into her door? Possibly, maybe there is one way to find out who did the deed. Other than a Russian having an assignment to kill The Snowman, of which Maxim would not be privy, Maxim was without a clue who could have made this attempt on his life. One thing he did know was that it was not a professional assassin nor anyone in that community, Russian or otherwise. The reason being, "The Snowman would be melted into nothing but a puddle of water," in layman's terms, Colin Cavanaugh would be dead!

He wanted a modus operandi to get as close to Abby as possible, and Maxim put out a few inquiries within his circle of friends and known operatives. Many of whom expressed much sorrow that The Snowman was merely injured in the attempt on his life. While waiting for replies to his request for information, Maxim could do nothing but be patient.

With no information coming his way, Maxim had one final avenue for an answer, and that was Nikolai, but why hasn't he gotten back to me? Wondering if the attempted shooting was professional; or as Maxim suspected it is personal. Knowing Colin's wife as I do, I would not be surprised if another one of her lovers wanted him dead. I am sure many want to eliminate the man. I can sympathize with their reasoning for doing so, but to actually kill another in the hopes of getting Abby is hard for me to wrap my head around. Reflecting on a recent conversation he had with Abby, she asked me to get rid of one of her lovers.

Maxim was having flashbacks of his intimate time with Abby; she was possibly one of the most alluring women he has ever met. Without regard to his feelings for Abby, he needed to take a step back from this drama and bow out of any further investigations before he found himself in jeopardy. That woman, no doubt, has some devil within. Then there is the profound chance her husband will recover, who knows what he may or may not offer regarding tracking down his assailant. The man is highly trained and can figure this out, and if this happened to me, I would go the distance to find out who tried to end my life.

Auggie and Diego were worried sick about Colin and but getting information firsthand was becoming remote and or not at all. Diego asked Auggie, "what will happen if the boss doesn't make it, Auggie?" Don't talk like that. He is a strong man, and Abby told us the surgery was a success, so now we wait and see what happens when he is fully awake. Diego, we need to focus on making this training the best we can in his absence and make Colin proud of our accomplishments. Of course, boss, I think we are doing an excellent job.

After Diego left the office, Auggie decided to check in on the guys; one, in particular, was Otto. Knowing anything could go wrong with this recruit, Auggie wanted to keep a close eye on Otto himself. Being watched by Erik again may not be wise. If Otto suspects him, it would be an international mess. Unknown to Auggie was that the entire encampment was under surveillance by the Russians with none other than Nikolai in charge. Otto was vital in getting the information Nikolai needed, but this assignment had its difficulties, one being *"who the hell shot Colin?"*

Nikolai knew he needed to respond to Maxim's text, but what should he say? He could not alert him about the assignment nor the reason. So avoidance seemed like a plan, but he knew Maxim well, he would suspect something was amiss if I didn't reply. I'm screwed if I do and more screwed if I don't. Shit, I hate having friends!

Maxim sees that his phone has a message, finally a return text from Nikolai. Reluctantly he opens the secure text message, "Maxim, I am amazed that you know nothing of the recent newsworthy reports regarding your friend." I am not available at present to meet. I am on an assignment of most importance. When complete, I will send a private message as to a time and place for a face to face meeting.

What the fuck! This message is so vague he might as well not have written it at all. What is going on that it appears I am in the dark? *Appears my ass, I am in the dark!* Furthermore, why is he assuming I care about "newsworthy" items. If I didn't know better, I would say he isn't involved in Colin's shooting and is just playing with me knowing that I am fishing for information, which of course, I am.

What an asshole friend he is during my time of need. What has happened to me, I'm acting like a rejected schoolboy by the high school's most popular girl.

So I have no information for Abby, this alone makes me appear inadequate. I only want to look perfect in her eyes, physically I am, but professionally at this moment, I look like a fool. Flash idea! What if I called Jim, surely he knows something? God, I hate talking to that man, but if he has any updated information he would share with me, it will make talking to Abby that much easier. I'll wait a bit and think about this next step before getting in touch with Jim. Best to have my ducks in a row.

Abby returned to the ICU after dinner in hopes that the nurse will have some promising news. The guard at the door alerts Abby that the doctor and his entourage are with Colin now, and she cannot go in until they come out. Panicked, Abby asked him if something happened? No, I don't think this is an emergency; I believe he is awake. Upset Abby asked, "Why didn't someone page me or call? I am his wife. I had a right to know." "Miss, I am assigned by the FBI to guard the door. I don't work for the hospital." Oh, I know, and I am sorry for carrying on like a nut. I understand he says, and this is a horrible situation. I think I will let them know you're out here how does that sound? Abby asked him, "by the way, what's your name? James, my name is James miss. Well, James, I would be very grateful if you would do that.

James, the guard, returned with news, "miss, they said you can go in now." Thank you so much for intervening on my part. No problem and I hope the news is good.

Nervous as hell, Abby slowly opens the door and, to her amazement, she saw Colin sitting up in bed with a huge smile on that handsome face. Darling, where have you been? Very funny pops first things first, doctor do you have an update. Yes, we do, and it is all good; he is a fortunate man. In what way is he lucky? Well, as of a few minutes ago, it was unknown if he would be able to walk now we know he can. With that news, Abby was in tears. Awe, darling come here; Colin asks Abby to sit next to him so he could give her a "hug." Oh, Colin, that is the best news ever, but how is your back? My lower back is sensitive and a little painful, but all in all, I feel terrific. What is the plan going forward, doctor? Rest and more rest, then once discharged, we will plan for physical therapy. Possibly in a week or two, he will be one hundred percent. Smiles all around!

As the doctor started to walk toward the door, he says to Colin, "young man, if it were not for the pristine physical condition you are in, I believe this would have ended badly, so whatever you do to stay that way keep doing it." Thanks, doc, now when will I be discharged? Another day or two at the earliest. You need to be able to walk a lot more stable than you are now, give it time, Mr. Cavanaugh.

Abby was happy but not so much, she knew she should have been, but she wasn't. Colin smiled with that honey "I'm innocent" smile; then Abby told him with a frown, "things need to change pops, not next year or next month nor next week they need to change now."

Oh darling, "if it weren't for bad luck, we'd have no luck at all." No pops, all of our bad luck was and is caused by you, by your business, no one to blame but you, and of course me for going along with it. If you can't make the necessary changes in your lifestyle, Colin, you and I are going to have a serious relationship conversation. Colin looked perplexed and disappointed, seeing his reaction Abby said, "that conversation is for another time pops it can wait until you are healed and recovered."

How about some real food pops? I'll get us a takeout from our favorite restaurant, how does that sound? That sounds wonderful, Abby; in the meantime, I feel fatigued. Take a nap, and I will be back here in an hour or two. She kisses Colin on the forehead and leaves.

Trying not to be pissed off, Colin mentally revisited how things went the last few months. His conclusion of the events of the past was indeed due to having his head up his ass and being love struct along with having developed an irresponsible way of doing business.

Wow, she is upset, maybe even mad; Abby's right, of course, both of us have suffered as a result of my falling in love. Who would have thought such a once in a lifetime love can cause all of this drama and turmoil? That cliché, "what's love got to with it." *Everything that's what!*

Colin thought about Abby threatened to leave him in Paris; he should have let her go. Heartbroken, he would have been, but they had a better chance of staying alive. Feeling sorry for himself, he drifted off for a much-needed rest.

Thank goodness Rachel, and Amanda brought her car to the hospital. Abby sat in the car for what seemed like forever. "I am such an ass." Who gives a sick person a tongue lashing like I did my husband? I meant every word of it, but the threats could have waited until he was home.

Oh well, what's done is done. *Unlucky, my ass!* Unquestionably Colin doesn't believe that? The man is delusional, Colin may be used to being attacked, kidnapped, shot at, and accosted, but I certainly am not. Well, not until I met him anyway!

Get going Abby, you have a long drive and round trip will take about two hours. What the hell was I thinking suggesting food from The Chateau? I do believe it will be a treat for Colin. Worth the drive to make amends for my inconsiderate behavior, even though I was right to do so.

The restaurant wasn't far from The Mall Bar; I think a drink and a few friendly faces are warranted. Abby parked her car and headed into her favorite happy hour place. Scoping the bar for anyone she may know, Abby walked straight to a barstool and sat down. Jack, the bartender, says. "well dang if it isn't our very own Abby Wells." Hey, Jack, how about a beer? How ya doing, Abby? I've been better for sure nothing a few drinks won't cure. Where is everyone, Jack? It's quite early, Abbs. They'll be round in a bit. Oh crap, it is early, isn't it Jack. Yep, here's your beer Abby.

Abby slowly sipped her beer, trying to relax when, to her joy, she saw Amy coming toward her.
"Abby Lynn, what the hell are you doing here, woman!" Oh, Amy, am I ever glad to see you, and with that, the tears started flowing. Abbs, let's get a table and have a "girl chat." The two friends moved to a table for some privacy. Now, what is going on, Abby, shouldn't you be at the hospital? I left to get us some dinner; Colin is resting. Oh, Amy, I am such an idiot, I lashed out at Colin before I left. I am so ashamed of doing that to a sick man. Abby, I'm sure if you did, you had a good reason. Yes, my intentions were solid, but my timing for getting it off my chest was wrong. What's done is done Abby, let it go for now.

Amy knew Abby had much on her mind. Trying not to be inconsiderate but needing to remind Abby of her upcoming wedding was important to her. Abby, "don't get upset with me, but, you do know our wedding is in two weeks, right?" Abby smiled and said, "how could I forget, I'm very excited to be a part of it, and I did get my dress altered." Thanks, Abby, that's one less thing to worry me. I need to leave Amy, but I'm so glad to have seen you and have this chat, I feel better already. Abby hugged her friend and left.

The Chateau restaurant was only a mile away from the mall; Abby got the carryout and headed for the hospital. She valet parked and headed straight for the room. Passing the gift shop, Abby decided to stop and get Colin a small gift. There it was a little teddy bear just like the one he got her when she was in the hospital. It was a sweet "I'm sorry for being an asswipe, gift."

Chapter 4

Maxim texted Jim and waited for his reply. Not convinced Jim had any more information than he did, but it was worth a try. Jim reluctantly returned Maxim's call, wondering what he wanted that could not wait until they were in the office. Jim, thanks for getting back to me. What's up, Maxim, that couldn't wait? Jim, "I'm getting bored, just sitting around. I need an assignment." You'll have one in the next day or so, have you finished your report on your last one? Yes, and I drop boxed it two days ago, Jim. Maxim was sweating now because he seriously had no viable reason to call Jim, and he must have sounded like an idiot.

So, Jim, how is the investigation into Mr. Cavanaugh's shooting going? And how does this concern you, Max? Jesus Jim, I'm only making small talk, maybe I could be of help? Jim was scratching his head, and a light goes off. With no leads himself, possibly Maxim could enter this investigation, but it would need to be incognito. Jim, you still there? Yes, give me a moment; I'm thinking. Alright, I will agree with you joining our investigation. But so we are clear on a few issues, one you will not discuss any information you may get with anyone, two you will not make any attempts to contact Abby Cavanaugh, understood? Of course, I do, and I had no intention of speaking to anyone, but you, this isn't my first rodeo Jim.

With that, Jim and Maxim agreed to exchange information. Maxim, of course, had nothing to tell, and neither did Jim. Both would keep that to themselves!

Jim was hopeful by allowing Maxim into his inner circle of friends; specifically, Colin and Abby wouldn't end up a mistake. But there was the possibility that he had contacts that could bring the suspect to the surface.

All parties now investigating the shooting included; Jim, Maxim, the FBI, Auggie, Joe, and the one who shouldn't be Abby.

All parties except Abby thought the same concept, and that was the shooting is personal, not professional. So why wasn't anyone talking about that to each other? Maybe because they didn't want to approach Colin, if they knew anything, it would be that if Colin knew he would not only want to know who, but why? Then he would merely eliminate the shooter from this world. All parties suspected the shooter was a prior or past lover, more than likely Abby's, but no one was talking.

No way in hell is anyone going up that road with The Snowman.

Abby returned to the hospital with their dinner and a teddy bear. When Abby got to the room, Colin had some visitor's his daughter and her husband. Maddie saw the look on Abby's face and said, "the baby is due any time now, but I wanted to see dad before I delivered." Oh, Maddie, I'm so glad you did, but I was surprised to see you here this close to your due date. It's not that far, and the drive took my mind off of the waiting.

I'm starving darling, did you bring my dinner. Yep, I did pops let me set it all on the tray for you. Maddie kissed her dad and said her goodbyes, then said she would call after the delivery. Abby told them they didn't need to leave that he could talk and eat at the same time. It's okay, Abby, we've been here for two hours, so it's time to go. Okay, Maddie, have a safe drive home, and then Abby hugged her.

Colin noticed that Abby seemed sad and asked her. "darling, does it upset you to see a pregnant woman ready to have a baby?" No pops it doesn't our baby wasn't meant to be born, and that is how it is, so no worries I'm good. Colin doubted that was an honest answer, but he accepted it anyway.

They both ate their dinner without much chatter and in solitude, way too quiet for him. Out of nowhere, Abby produced a small package on his tray. Hey, what's this, Abby? A gift for you pops, open it. Colin smiled, "darling, thank you; I've always wanted a tiny teddy bear." Pops, you are an ass sometimes. Oh, Abbs, I was only kidding. Now come closer so I can try to kiss you. Abby moves towards the bed but hesitates for a moment. Something wrong, darling, you don't want to kiss me anymore. Oh, for heaven's sake, Colin, of course, I do. Why did you hesitate, then? I was thinking about something, that's all.

Colin accepted her reply but didn't buy into it for one minute.

Colin, I want to ask you a question, and I want a straight answer. Always darling now what's up with you tonight? "I want to know who shot you and why?" Abby Lynn, "my honest answer is I have no fucking idea." None pops? Well, l have no one specific person in mind, but as you well know, it could have been someone I did business with or anyone related to a past incident. Darling, this is not the time to have this conversation; let's wait until I go home. Fine, but, as soon as you're feeling better, we will revisit this. Absolutely, and are you staying tonight or going home? If it's okay with you, I would like to sleep in my bed tonight.

Abby leaves the hospital with so many thoughts and questions she's overwhelmed with all of this drama in her life. I need a drink again, and that is not a good thing. Overthinking all of her ideas has not helped with her search for the truth. No drinking tonight, once I get home, I will make some notes and start a plan of action.

Colin was deep in thought after Abby left, what is going on with my life? Ideas are running amok, and my thoughts are unhinged, to say the least. How am I going to get business back to what it used to be without messing up my marriage of oh let me see a month or less? My head hurts with lost faith that I once had as the say goes, "I need my groove back." Managing life pre-Abby was fruitful and productive; life post-Abby is a non-balance of love and heartbreak.

Woe is me and stop the whining, Colin!

Maxim was thrilled to be "formally" involved in the Colin and Abby drama. As if I wasn't connected via Abby and using my lust for her as a means to an end wasn't evil enough. That thought alone leans me toward this shooting is a personal vendetta, but against whom, Abby or Colin. What I needed was a way to convince Nikolai to let me get embroiled into his assignment, which I am sure has everything to do with The Snowman.

Connecting with Nikolai so soon seemed unnecessary, and Maxim felt it would jeopardize his pursuit of information. It can wait!

Gabriel Gennaro had his GPS set and was en route to Colin's house. Who would have thought in a million years I would be investigating the president-owner of our company? This assignment is life-changing, if I find wrongdoing, I'm fucked, and if I don't catch the culprit, I am also fucked. Why me? Stop being such a pussy GG and get the job done, and may the chips fall where they do.GG heard that his wife went home for the night, so he headed in that direction. It's hard to believe Mr. Cavanaugh lives in this small town and in such a small home. Considering his house on the lake is worth millions, why don't they live there. Rumor has it that Colin loves his wife so much that he is nearly out of reach with reality. I say, "no way, no how is that true."

GG arrived at their house a little after nine o'clock, so the lights were on. When Abby answered the door, she was sure it would be Joe, disappointment showed on her face. Well, alrighty, then GG said, "I'm usually greeted with more joy." Sorry I was expecting someone else. Let's start fresh, Mrs. Cavanaugh; my name is Gabriel Gennaro. I am an investigator looking into your husband's shooting. May I come in? Identification, please? He was so hoping she wouldn't ask, but now that she has, he had no choice but to…… lie.

GG showed her his Private Investigator license; this way, his real employer was kept secret. Fine, please come in. Gabriel could see that possibly they were moving a tip-off since boxes lay everywhere. Mrs. Cavanaugh, I have a few questions on behalf of my client. Abby looking directly into his eyes, asked, "who sir is your client?" I'm afraid that it is confidential. Really, that sounds, "so tv drama, and I am not buying it." I see he says, "well I have one question for you, do you want to find the person or persons responsible for hurting your husband" and "to prevent them from trying again?"

Abby thought long and hard on how to answer this question without sounding like she didn't care. Carefully she replies, "only an ass wouldn't want to bring this person to justice, especially me." GG then asked. "can I have your full cooperation on this case?"

Abby was sizing the guy up, young and handsome, confident and smart, along with manipulative. I like him already!

May I offer you a drink, Gabriel? What is your beverage of choice Mrs. Cavanaugh? I'm having a glass of wine; a Chablis will that do? Very much so, indeed, thanks. Abby poured herself and her guest a drink and then sat down next to him, evidently for a show of intimidation. Caught off guard with that move, GG did not move an inch; he merely smiled at the fact that his home office hit the nail on the head about her confidence level. *Ain't this gonna be fun!*

So, Mr. Gennaro, what would you like to ask? Please call me GG, everyone does. Okay, as long as you call me, Mrs. Cavanaugh. Damn this woman is intimidating as hell, why does she sit so close? My questions are along the line of developing a timeline for the last few weeks. Or even months. Wow that may take a long time, and it is so late, might I offer a better way to go about doing this task? Hold on a minute, I need to make a copy of a document, and while I'm at it, I will pour us another glass. Perplexed and in awe of this woman, how is it that some men can snatch a hottie like this one, and I can't even get a date. I've heard all the gossip and rumors regarding her beauty. All of which isn't rumor anymore because she is all of that and more. Keep your pants on GG you aren't so shabby, and I could see her looking me over. Abby handed him his glass of wine along with a few pieces of paper. What is this? You wanted a timeline for Colin, and so here it is. When did you have time to do this? While he was in surgery and the recovery room.

Amazed, he glanced at it and said he would review it later. Is there anything else I can help you with GG? Would you have thought to add names and contact information? Mr. Gennaro, I am a very detailed woman. I don't forget much, everything you need from me is on those sheets. Did you eat dinner? What, uhm no, not really. Are you hungry? Confused and scared to death to say no or even yes all of a sudden, his mouth opened and said, "yes, I am famished, thank you."

Shit, I need to get out of here like now! No wonder the boss is crazy about this woman; she is something else.

Abby knew she was driving that man crazy and deliberately so. She was smiling as she headed into the kitchen to fix them a sandwich. When she returned, Mr. Gabriel Gennaro was nowhere to be found.

That was so much fun. I can't stop laughing!

Abby was in a much better mood now taking a hot bath would do wonders, then she would take her notes and figure out a way to find the shooter.

Chapter 5

Blake was sick with worry; Rachel was not helping his situation at all. I want to say she means well, but that would be a lie. Rachel is nothing but a conniving little bitch and not at all like her mother. Even though it has only been a few days since he last talked to Abby, he wanted to try.

Abby answered her phone, "you should be sleeping and not calling me." I cannot sleep because I wanted to hear your voice, Abby Lynn. Jesus Blake, I thought you were Colin. I told you not to call until things settled down. I can't help myself, and you know it. I know you can't help how you feel Blake, but you did catch me in a good mood. Excellent, can I come over? No, I'm not in that good of a spirit, although I am feeling quite frisky. Don't tease me, Abbs, I can't take you teasing me. If you sneak in the back door, you can come over for a drink, but only a drink. I 'm ready for bed, so you'll need to forgive my attire. Forgiven, and I am on my way.

Blake did the happy dance with moves he hardly ever got to make; she always plays hard to get, so why was tonight so easy? Who cares, not me that's who?

Taking his new therapist's advice, he bought all new clothes, got an updated hairstyle, and even new shoes. Feeling extremely confident that this visit would end with him and Abby in bed having great sex.

Abby has a plan, and that plan starts by eliminating suspects one at a time.

Reviewing her notes for a starting point, she hoped to cross off Blake's name tonight. Would her plan backfire if allowing herself to seduce Blake to a confession if he had one? Or would it be fruitful by him having some useful information to offer by leaving the seduction off the table? He will confess, or he will suffer! Poor guy, he couldn't bear any more than he already has.

Abby knew it was true, but she also believed he would talk. Talk or walk; those were his only options tonight. Being a "hard ass" was almost laughable to Abby, but try she must.

GG was still in the neighborhood; whatever had possessed him to hang around, he wasn't sure, but the feeling felt good. Meaning his instincts told him watching that woman could lead to clues and or the culprit. Anything was possible, and nothing was not.

Blake tapped ever so lightly on the back door. Abby was waiting for him with a glass of wine and a very lovely see-through nightie. Drive the man crazy, seduce, and then go for the interrogation.

Blake was in awe by the vision in front of him and his luck. Abby didn't give him the chance to touch her, let alone wait for a kiss. He happily followed her into the living room. Abby sat down and handed Blake a glass of wine as she patted the sofa cushion indicating this was where she wanted him to sit. Ever so hesitant, Blake thinks to himself, "something's up; that's for sure." He knew Abby better than anyone on this planet, even her husband.

Abby, not to question your personal indulgences, but what the hell is up with you tonight? Why Blake, whatever do you mean? What I mean is, "this display of seduction is wonderful, but it is not you, Abby." So what are you saying, "you don't want to be seduced by me? Nor do you want to make love to me?" You know I do, but something feels out of place. Sit down Blake and stop being so melodramatic. Maybe inviting you over was a mistake; possibly, I did so in a moment of weakness.

Please sit-down Blake; you're making me very uncomfortable. He sat down, knowing he was melting fast, not caring what her motivation was any longer. Abby Lynn, you know I love you. Yes, I do, but you haven't even kissed me, and I am very disappointed, Blake. Sorry Abby, but I'm confused by your attitude tonight; you're acting somewhat strange. Good God Blake I'm practically throwing myself at you, I want you and all you've done is complain.

You've changed Blake. I'm not sure I like the "new you." Sorry Abbs, can we start over? I don't see the point you have ruined my night and my desires. *Oh, brother Abby!* I was lonely, Blake I needed a friend, a close friend I wanted some loving company. I wanted you, Blake, just you. Abby knew she had him right where she needed him, feeling guilty for acting like an ass, and now he was hers. She gave him a frown like a little puppy dog look, and it broke his heart.

All of a sudden, Blake stands up, putting his glass on the table he motioned with his hand for Abby to take. Abby stood up and waited for the famous Blake ritual of carrying her to the bedroom. When they got upstairs, she motioned with her head towards the spare bedroom; he looked surprised. Blake places Abby on the bed and then excuses himself to freshen up. When he returns, Abby did not disappoint by being entirely bare and uncovered on top of the quilt.

Abby Lynn, you are breathtakingly beautiful. Lay with me, Blake, and hold me. Blake pulls her close, but she doesn't respond as she usually does. Please go slow and just hold me for a few minutes. He doesn't only want to hold his love; he wants to make love; he starts kissing and moves his hand across every inch of her body. Abby asked Blake if he missed her. Of course, I miss seeing you, and I try not to because you've made it clear how you feel. You know that's not what I want Blake but how it has to be for now. All these external obstacles in my life have caused me to make changes, but finally, I believe things are changing.

Blake sat up, "what are you saying, Abby?" Meeting Colin has not been a bed of roses Blake, sometimes I fear for my life. You're exaggerating Abby; he wouldn't allow that. "So you say but not the case Blake."

What the hell Abby what's going on? I don't want to talk about it, especially right now. Now is good Abby right fucking now is a good time. Calm down! No, I will not calm down I don't want you to be in jeopardy Abby or the girls. What if you would have been with him at the airport, you could have been shot as well or killed.

Abby sat straight up so she could look him in the eye. "How did you know the shooting took place at the airport?" At that, Blake knew he had fucked up and badly. Oh, it was in the paper I saw it. No, it was not Blake. *Blake Thomason, how did you know?* Shit!

Get out of my house now! Abby grabbed her robe and left Blake to dress. When he got to the kitchen, he found her sitting in a dining chair crying. How could you? How could I what Abby, what are you saying? You! It was you who shot my husband! Wait a minute Abbs. I did no such thing, and you know that; I love you, Abby, you also know I'm no killer. Jesus, I cannot believe you think I'm capable of killing someone. Blake is so appalled by Abby's accusations he has to sit before he falls.

How did you know Blake? Blake knew the truth would hurt Abby, but if he didn't talk, he knew he would never see her again. I heard it somewhere or saw it on tv or something. Hell no, you are lying to me Blake I can feel it. Oh, Abby, please, this is ridiculous because you know it wasn't me, and right now, you are breaking my heart. She wasn't going to back off, and he knew it, so he had no choice but to tell her, and then she would be heartbroken forever.

With all the rage she could fester out of her body, she backed Blake into the wall of her kitchen and threatened him once more. Blake had never seen this side of Abby. Forcing him against the wall with her body Abby felt a strength so powerful that Blake shouted "stop" okay.

Tell me now where you got that information.

It was from Rachel! Rachel told me, Abby.

The shock on Abby's face frightened him so much that he

broke out in a sweat. He couldn't think of a thing to say that would lighten the blow of a child's betrayal. Blake saw that she was wavering and had become unsteady so much so that Blake placed her into a chair for fear she would fall. After a few minutes, she said, "I want to know every word she told you, don't leave out anything, not a single word. I want to know how she knew, who told her. And how you got the information from my daughter."

I want the truth, and if I think I don't have the truth, you will be dead to me forever.

Nikolai wanted to leave Costa Rica in the worst way. There is no one of interest here, no one of importance, so why stay. Sometimes he disagreed with his superiors; obviously, this is one more version of that. Colin is in the hospital; no one from any American agency is in this camp. Yes, there is a possible contact within the trainees, but I have already connected with him in hopes of recruitment into our group. So far, he has shown no interest, but I have been instructed to convince him otherwise. The remaining two men running the show here are insignificant and of no importance whatsoever.

Bored is what I have become, and I am tired of ignoring the text messages from my friend Maxim. Why is he so interested in the shooting of The Snowman? My take on that is it's a woman, and my guess is she is Cavanaugh's wife. I do not believe Maxim so stupid that he would try to kill The Snowman. No way it was him, Maxim would not have missed the shot of that, I am sure.

The extreme's some men go to for love is overwhelmingly ill-advised by my standards. One can find pleasure and the company of a woman without the idea of love. God knows I'm an expert in that game. Falling this hard for any woman is something I never thought Maxim would allow. He can have any woman he wants, why Mrs. Cavanaugh? I have seen her, and without a doubt, she is an exceptional woman in many ways, not only beautiful, but I have heard she is also cunning and smart. More

LYNDA L FREEMAN

the reason to beware, but I think not in Maxim's case.

Once bitten, twice shy! Of this, my friend, you should adhere.

Chapter 6

Nikolai made his decision to connect with Maxim before Maxim tried him yet again. When Maxim saw the text, he was pleasantly pleased and appreciative that his friend knew that he was needed. To Nikolai's amazement, Maxim didn't want to talk; he wanted to meet and as soon as possible. Because Maxim needed my help? Nikolai has never known Maxim to ask anyone for help; this request was unusual. Nikolai replied with, "Конечно, мы можем встретиться.", ("of course we can meet.") Nikolai said he would come to the states if Maxim wanted but would prefer to meet in Berlin.

Berlin, there is no way I can go to Germany to meet. Return text, "Ник я не могу встретиться из страны, пожалуйста, приезжайте в Америку, Чикаго". ("Nik I cannot meet out of the country, please come to America, Chicago.") reply soon?

Four days Max, no sooner! Nikolai knew Maxim had no idea where he was nor his current assignment. So the arrangements were made to meet in Chicago in four days and that Nikolai would text when he arrived. Maxim was pleased, but he also knew the possibility existed that Nik also had other reasons for coming. Those reasons would surface soon enough, but until then, Maxim could only speculate why Nikolai so willingly agreed to meet. Visiting in America is risky for any foreign intelligence officer, but a Russian agent more so than most.

It was late and at two a.m. Blake walked out Abby's back door with his head hanging low so low in fact that he sloughed over like an old man. Swearing to himself with every step, he'd had enough. Defeated and now a broken man Blake knew it was over. A few tears dropped from his swollen red eyes into his mouth, leaving a salty taste, right then he vowed never to see Abby again.

Well, well, what a man can see if he waits long enough. Gabriel's instincts were spot on, Mrs. Cavanaugh reeked of suspicious behavior. Now, what reason would a married woman have to let a handsome young man leave her home by the back door? Bingo! She doesn't want anyone to see him. The bigger question is, why?

Abby was still in disbelief, and as a mother, she didn't want to believe a word that came from Blake's mouth. No one knew Blake as well as she did; she knew he was telling the truth. How is it possible I could have two daughters so different? Abby knew Rachel had a dark side, but to betray one's own mother was deployable and an unforgivable act.

Being upset with Blake was understandable but mostly because he more than likely would never have told me the truth. There were, of course, many reasons for him not to divulge the facts, too many to think about tonight. Notwithstanding Blake's forced confessions, Abby knew deep down he would never have told her if for no other reason than he knew Rachel could be in serious trouble if caught. So many people were diligently looking for the shooter, the FBI, local police, and the TSA hell even me, not to mention the guy from Centry Security.

After much thought, Abby suspected that she had an idea who may be involved. She had to get to the culprits right away, but one was incarcerated, and the other was incognito finding them and getting them to talk would take some doing.

Knowing sleep would not come easy, and with only a few hours left until dawn, Abby grabbed the bottle of pills next to the bed. Reading the label on Colin's prescription, Abby thought about only taking half a sleeping pill but decided what the hell and swallowed the whole thing.

Colin was getting quite agitated, wondering why Abby wasn't there yet. He was sure he would be released and soon. Wanting to call her to see where the hell she was, as he picked up the phone next to his bed, he realized as he laughed to himself, I don't know her number. Where the fuck is my cell phone? Great, so much for "speed dialing" Abby put her number in my phone months ago, all I did was hit the number two and there she was.

Colin called the office, and Joe answered, "Joe, don't laugh, but I need to call Abby, what's her number?" It was all Joe could do to stifle laughing, but he knew Colin wouldn't think it funny. Where's your cell phone, Colin? Hell if I know Joe that's a worry for sure, see if you can track it down using the GPS feature. Now please give me Abby's numbers.

Groggy as hell Abby answered the phone with a barely audible "hello." Abby Lynn, "what the hell, were you sleeping?" Colin, "oh my gosh, what time is it?" Almost ten darling, why are you still in bed? Are you ill? No pops I couldn't sleep, so when I was still awake at two a.m. I was desperate for rest, so I took one of your sleeping pills. Abby, those are for a large man, not a tiny ass woman. Well, regardless, I slept well, didn't I?

Just when I thought I could trust you by yourself, darling. Very funny pops! Darling, are you coming to get me, or should I call Joe? Are you being released? Yes, I believe, so the doctor was in earlier and said he had to finish his rounds, then he would do the paperwork. Fantastic news pops as soon as I get showered and dressed; I'll be there.

Jim finally received the CCTV tapes from the TSA. When he saw how many there were, he knew he needed help viewing them. They have tapes of all areas of the airport, which meant hours visually looking for the shooter. Jim decided to call Maxim to help, Max was already involved, so Jim felt comfortable with him helping, but he wanted no one to see these tapes, even his director Marilyn. Jim feared this shooter could be someone other than a professional. Yes, he was right and knew it was no one in the business, or Colin would be dead.

Assassins don't miss their mark!

Maxim surprised that Jim asked for his help but agreed too. Not that he had much choice in the matter Jim was his superior, which in every way possible Maxim hated.

Abby was shocked; she slept so late but delighted she did. Sleep deprivation was not an option. I need to be on my best game face, and for that, I need rest. Abby ignored the fact that soon, she would need to see Rachel. But there were many issues to contend with and people to see before confronting her daughter. Abby wanted, needed to hear Rachel's version of the events leading up to the shooting. I can't overreact to anything I need to stay focused on the task at hand.

My daughters are so different, Rachel was fearless and reckless, Amanda was bold and smart. Being fearless and reckless makes me nervous about my daughter's future, but in this case, I would say she had some outside help and direction to accomplish this heinous act.

With no time last night to review Blake's version of what Rachel told him, Abby was of the mindset that possibly Rachel confessed to Blake knowing he would tell me. Let this go for now Abby Lynn because the devils in the details so I will wait for Rachel's story.

GG managed to get a few hours of sleep; it would have to do. He knew he had to error on the side of caution with this information; his livelihood depended on it. His job would be judged on facts and being able to prove them. With the photo he took of the man, he hoped to identify him using facial recognition software. This process would take time, but if the mystery man were on any public social media or news articles, he would be known. GG knew he would have the man's name by the end of the day. His job was not to be a judge or jury but to lay out the facts to the right people.

Abby finally arrived at the hospital; she put on her happy face for her husband. She could not give away her anxiety or concerns with last night's drama. Eventually, Colin would find out on his own. He always did.

Darling, I have been officially discharged. I have all the doctor's orders, and I am ready to go home. Abby, I feel so lucky to be alive and blessed to have you, darling. Let's see if we can go longer than a few weeks without any shootings, kidnapping, or drama of any kind. Oh, pops, you are so melodramatic! No drama is what we need, Abby; let's go home.

Abby had the cleaning service clean while she went to get Colin. Rose Abby's mom made a casserole for lunch and put flowers on the table. She wanted Colin to come home to a clean, comfortable home and some food to eat.

The house looks nice darling, and I am famished, so how about some non-hospital food? Alright pops first things first, let me take a look at your instructions from the doctor. Why? What do you mean, "why?" Abby, I am not a child and am more than capable of managing my healthcare.

Right then, the doorbell chimes!

Who in the hell could that be pops no one knew we were coming home? Abby opens the door to find none other than "nurse Joe." Ha, I should have known you two were in cahoots. The patient needs a nurse, so here I am ready, willing, and able to serve. Hilarious Joe, will you be staying long? Long as I'm needed, Abby and all kidding aside, I want to help. Well, regardless, we're happy you're here and appreciate your help, Joe. No overnights through I can handle that part. Now can I see my patient? This way, Joe, he's, of course, eating so nothing wrong with his appetite. Hospital food sucks, as we all know.

Blake booked his flight to Madrid he would visit for an extended length of time or at least until he could forget about Abby. Knowing that soon, Abby would speak with Rachel, and that would be more than he could bear, so leaving was his way of avoiding or dealing with the situation. It was all too painful.

Blake knew Rachel could be in harm's way and or worse legal trouble. Even though she did not do the deed, she was the originator of the plan. Her accomplices were happy to partake of the idea and went forward using her as a scapegoat. I suspect Rachel was merely speaking to them about how much she disliked

Colin; then, they took it from that point. They all knew Colin could have been a target by any villains, and knowing this is why they thought the shooter would never be caught.

Other than knowing how and who was involved, Blake knew nothing before the shooting; he only becomes privy after the fact. Young girls and drinking is not a good idea. Blake already misses his love of a lifetime, but with time and much therapy, he would overcome his heartache.

What a crock of crap! The chances of that happening are zero!

Joe asked Colin to let him see the information the doctor gave him. You're as bad as Abby; the two of you are nosey and interfering as hell. The list Colin, otherwise, I can't help you get well. Oh well, here it is, but I'm not promising I will follow his advice. At that point, Abby intervened, "you will do exactly as the doctor orders pops." Are the two of you going to double team on me for the duration of my recovery? Abby and Joe nodded in agreement, "yes, we are."

Colin excused himself to take a nap, he wouldn't be sleeping but instead needed to make some phone calls in private. Reviewing his notes, Colin called his investigator, GG. To his surprise, it appeared he did have some leads and wanted to talk to Colin in person. That's not possible, Gabriel unless you come to my home. Okay, let me get my things and paperwork together? Come by tomorrow Gabriel early. I want Abby to hear what you have.

Gabriel wasn't sure he was ready to share with Colin just yet. He needed the identity of the man in the photo first. His thought process was I'll report all else and wait on the other.

Abby wanted to share the information she had with Joe but decided not to. I think Joe would want Colin to know the information out of loyalty or encourage me to tell him. I'm not ready to tell anyone what I know because I need to speak with Rachel first. Again being married to Colin is so complicated and full of crazy events. The cost of our relationship may end up being more than I care to pay.

Colin called Auggie to give him an update and to let him he was home and on the mend. Auggie asked Colin, "have you caught the person who did this?" No, and Auggie, I am amazed that thus far, no one nor any agency has a lead. That's is very disturbing boss. Diego and I were wondering who messed up a hit leaving you alive to hunt them down. Auggie, "you know I will find out who did this to me." I do not doubt that, boss! Everything is good here, so no worries, the end of the training will be in a few days, so I can't see any reason for you to return. No, Auggie, I will not be able to be there, but I will do the exit interviews via video streaming device. I owe the class at least that, and I am going to offer at a later time a one-on-one class for each student. Colin, I will overnight all of the details for each member so you can see their progress. "My only concern is regarding Otto Zimmerman, " and I believe that he is a plant and, more than likely, a member of a Russian Agency. Auggie, I will take care of Otto; just let him go about his business as if we know nothing about him. Got it, boss, I will email the information you need.

Chapter 7

Abby made a few phone calls herself while supposedly Colin was resting. She left Rachel a message that she wanted to see her as soon as possible. Hopefully, her daughter hasn't figured out that I am aware of the facts. How could Rachel not know that Blake would eventually confide in me? Surely she knows he is not a person who keeps secrets from the person he loves.

Next, Abby calls Blake to see if he has had a change of heart regarding her using him to get whatever she could from him. It was not a task Abby felt good about, and she wanted to tell him that very thing. Abby knew Blake was upset with her methods of discovery, and he even went so far as to say he was never going to speak to her again. She thought he said that at the time, due to being angry with her, but little did she know how serious he was. Abby wasn't sure she was ready for Blake to be out of her life altogether; the thought sort of made her uneasy inside.

Blake's landline and his cell phones had the same announcement, "please leave a message, and I will return your call at my earliest convenience, I am out of town for an extended leave of absence." What the hell is he up too? Abby was quite concerned and called again to be sure she heard it correctly. Is it possible he is so upset with me that he left town? Good lord, what have I done? Abby left a message because, at this point, that was all she could do. Thoughts of immediately driving to his house, which is not possible.

Blake finished closing up the house and went next door to his neighbor, giving him contact information just in case there was an emergency. Blake told him he was not to tell anyone his whereabouts and or to pass along any information. Packing as much as he could get into three suitcases was all he could do on such short notice. The realtor said the vacation villa had every-thing needed for the perfect stay. Blake hated to leave, but it has been many years since he took a trip. Now that he decided to go, Blake was getting excited to be doing so. He decided on the Catalonia region, with lively beach resorts of Costa Brava, all this per the travel agent.

Other than Abby-has Blake ever done anything exciting? Not that he could recall.

GG still has not heard from the company he used to find the mystery man. There was no way to use Centry Security; that's for sure. No secret's within a security company. He was notified by the home office that Colin was out of the hospital and wanted to speak with him. This information was of no importance because he already knew Colin was home.

Amy and David had some last-minute details to work out for their wedding, so they decided to go to happy hour. David suggested they make a few calls to see who else could go, hell we might as well have a pre-wedding party. Amy loved the idea and started making calls. Doubting Abby could go, but she called her anyway. Abbs, "we're all headed to the Mall Bar, can you meet us?" Amy, I would love to, Colin's home now, so let me check hold on a minute. Abby talks to Colin, who thinks she should go and not to worry because Joe is there, and they will be fine without her. Amy, "what time are you going?" Five, we're meeting at five. Great I will see you there.

Abby certainly needed a diversion from the hectic and dramatic life she leads as Mrs. Cavanaugh. Meeting her friends was an escape she looked forward to enjoying. Unfortunately, there was very little about her life she could share with them. Who in the hell would believe any of it anyway? Abby made Colin some lunch while Joe took care of his nurse duties. Colin needed and wanted his life back to normal as soon as possible.

Normal? What the hell is that?

Jim and Maxim have neck aches and vision issues as a result of viewing the many digital tapes of the airport. Maxim spoke first, "Jim, are these the only CCTV cameras in the airport?" These are the ones that were closest to the escalator Colin was on when hit. Then we must have missed something, or the shooter averted the cameras. That seems to make sense, but in reality, it does not, the shooter is on these films somewhere. Let's start the process over using the trajectory of how we think the bullet traveled from point A point to B. Good idea let me get the report from the TSA.

No longer viewing separately, they sat together and looked for anyone suspicious in the film they thought was the right one. All of a sudden, Jim does a double-take, and Maxim asks, "Jim, did you see someone?" Holy shit, stop the tape and back it up a frame or two. Slowly Maxim moves the cursor to the left. Stop! The look on Jim's face was an unbelievable surprise. Well, well, who do we have here? Maxim was so perplexed he just stared at Jim with a "what the hell do you see look, and are you going to share it with me?" Jim stared at the frame for what seemed to be forever. Earth to Jim, what are you seeing?

Maxim, Jim says, "see the guy in the hoodie and black pants and a baseball hat on?" Yes, do you know this person? Oh, I most definitely do! Okay, are you going to tell me, or should I guess? Max, you don't know this man, but I do, he is one of the men involved with Abby's ex-husband. He was tangled up in Abby's abduction last year. Runs with the wrong crowd but went with the prosecutor on a lesser charge, so no jail-time. Why the hell would he want to shoot Colin? That my friend can be summed up in one sentence. Someone paid him to do it! Let's continue watching and see if it shows him firing the shots. Frame by frame, they focus their eyes on the screen until bingo there it is Luke aiming his weapon in the direction of the escalator. Jim yells, "busted again, asshole."

Tell me the story, Jim, before I die a slow death waiting. Jim proceeds to tell Maxim about the incident involving Abby's ex and her friends. Jesus Jim, does the drama ever stop for these two? They do seem to be plagued with one crisis after another. Would this Luke character think of doing this on his own? Hell no, he's an idiot with some skills we didn't know he had. Doesn't take much ability to shoot and miss Jim, then Max laughs.

If I had to guess Max, I would bet her ex Ed Wells thought up this plan to get even with her and Colin. Isn't Abby's ex in prison? He is indeed, but when has that stopped an inmate from getting help from the outside. What is your next step, Jim? That's something I need to think long and hard about Max. My thoughts precisely because I would not want Colin Cavanaugh coming for me!

Rachel listened to her mom's message and wondered what could be so urgent. She already knew Colin, unfortunately, was released and home. I swear the man has nine lives! Mom doesn't know about my hand in this conspiracy, so why am I feeling reluctant to return her call.

Abby answered her phone on the first ring. "mom, what up?" Rachel, I need to speak with you as soon as we can meet. Wow, mom, you could have at least said "hello" first. No, Rachel, I am not in a sociable mood, so again, when can you meet me? How about tomorrow for breakfast? I can stop by the house before classes. No, I want to meet somewhere else, not here. What the hell, mom, why? You'll know when we talk, meet me at Ginny's at eight am. Fine mom, I will see you there, and I hope you will be in a better mood. That's doubtful Rach very doubtful indeed.

Jesus, what the fuck is her problem! Rachel was beginning to wonder if Abby knows. Nah, how would she ever find out? Dad would never boast about this because he knows how much trouble I would be in not only with mom but the police. But what else could have mom so upset? Shit, I need to get in touch with my father. Rachel called Luke on the burner phone they bought. Rach, "you should not be calling me." I know what we agreed on Luke, but somethings come up. Like what? Mom wants to meet me for a chat, and not at her house. Luke, she was upset with me; I could sense she was mad. Calm down, Rachel; there is no way she could know.

So says you and I am calling dad or going up to see him, do you want to go? Hell no, we do not need to be seen together. Rachel, you need to watch what you do and how you act; our lives depend on it. Easy for you to say, but I did tell you that my mom is smart and has friends in the right places. Rachel, no one is going to find out what happened. Just hear what your mom has to say, and then we will see if we need to make other plans. Luke, "what the hell does that mean?" Nothing, Rachel, call me after you see your mom. *Admit nothing!*

Amanda wanted to see for herself how mom and Colin were handling all of this drama. So she asked if she could come over for dinner and to do laundry. Abby welcomed the chance to talk with Amanda before seeing Rachel.

Colin was well-rested, medicated, and ready to get out of the damn bed. Immediately he smells something good in the kitchen. My, my, darling, what are you cooking? Dinner, are you hungry? You know I am when will this feast be ready? In about an hour and Amanda is joining us, won't that be nice. "What about Rachel, Abby?" I just talked to her she said she has an exam tomorrow, so she needs to study. Hum that never stopped her before. I'm only telling you what she said, Colin.

It was late for dinner, but Abby wanted to do something special, she felt guilty for meeting her friends for happy hour, but it did put her in a better mood and some normalcy.

It was all Abby could do to keep her composure as Colin put his arms around her waist and pulled her close. Kissing her on the neck, Darling, "I have missed being close to you, holding you." oh pops, it's hard to stay positive and have faith that our lives will become somewhat normal. I know Abby, but believe me, that is my number one goal going forward. Now is not the time for many reasons, but as soon as I am healed and back to work, my plans for change will take place. I live for the day Colin and that you are serious about these changes. I am not sure I can take much more tragedy happening to us. You have my word, darling; the day will come and soon. That is why I went to Chicago.

I have already started the process with my executive board. Do you promise pops? Yes, my decisions did not go well with most; but when I finalize my plans, I think they will all be happy.

How about a glass of wine before dinner Abby? Colin, I don't think drinking is a good idea. To hell with that, I want to have a drink with my girl. I've already had two beers at the Mall, or did you forget? I think I slept through that, and I didn't miss you at all. Very funny pops just wait until you're ready for some action I'll show you how much I missed you. And I live for that day, darling.

Amanda arrived and was pleased to see Colin up and trying to walk. She thought he looked older and sickly, which of course, he was. Amanda gave Colin a peck on the cheek and her mom as well. Something smells wonderful mom. I'm starving. Good because I got carried away with this cooking idea.

Sipping their wine, it appeared as life ordinary. Joe had started a fire before he left, which felt warm and happy for a change. Colin sat next to Abby but fidgeted now and then due to his back hurting. Amanda asked, "Colin, what is the timeframe for your injuries to heal?" Joe told me today it would take weeks to get back to normal, whatever that means. "Does it hurt much, Amanda asks?" Only when I move or walk or stand, but I will not let this stop me from going about my business, I am not one to be bedridden.

Dinner's ready, let's eat! Sitting at the dining room table, Abby looked at Colin and her daughter and thanked God for this night. No drama, no interference from anyone, just a peaceful dinner with family, and she missed Rachel but not her bad decisions.

Abby was not looking forward to tomorrow.

Chapter 8

Colin and Abby snuggled themselves to death; it has been a long time since they slept together in their bed, in their home. Abby asked her husband if he thought they would have happier times soon? Darling, I do, but I am surprised you would ask me a question like that. Abby, you know, as well as I do that, we have many events coming up that will make you smile and be happy. Amanda's graduation, the wedding, and soon we will move into our new home. So you see things could be worse. I'm not sure that is possible pops, but I want to remain positive. Good, we need to see that glass half full darling. I'm trying Colin, I genuinely am.

Abby Lynn, you know I want to make love to you. I want to love all of you, show you how much I love and cherish you, darling. Abby started to say something, but he put his finger on her lips, stopping her from speaking. Let me finish Abby. I know this was not what you expected when our relationship began, and that is partly due to my unwillingness to share my secrets with you or anyone. My business can be a risky business and dangerous at times, as you now know. But darling most of what I do, and my company does is not harmful or risky. Yes, I have done some risky, perilous things in my life, but all of that is behind me. That shit is for a younger man than me. I will not be putting our lives in jeopardy any longer.

Abby kissed Colin on his forehead, then his nose, and then his lips. She moved down to his chest, which she thought was the sexiest chest she had ever seen. Abby Lynn, this is not a good idea. I did just get released from the hospital, remember. Shush pops; you don't need to move your back or anything else just enjoy.

Pain and agony could not feel any better!

Abby woke up truly refreshed and ready to face the day and whatever events it brought. None of the events of the past year was her fault, nor were they caused by her. That includes the Jaci debacle. Abby decided she was no longer blaming herself, no more wallowing in regrets, and ill will. From a crazy ex-husband to her betraying friends and even Colin's livelihood, none of it was her fault. Abby knew she did not want to be a magnet for a crisis any longer.

Abby called Colin to get his butt down for breakfast. When he didn't run for food, she became worried. Darn, what the hell is he doing up there? Then Colin hobbled into the kitchen like an older man in pain. "Pops, are you okay?" Do I look okay to you, darling? No, you don't, so do you want me to take you back to the hospital? No Joe will be here in a few minutes, he'll think of something to relieve the pain. Colin, did you take the pain meds they gave you. No, and I probably won't; they're addictive, I want nothing to do with them.

Colin ate a fair amount of breakfast, and then Abby helped him to a chair, so he was more comfortable. I texted Joe to see what time we could expect him. His response was he was on his way. Pops I hate seeing you in pain is there something I can do to help. Not really, Abby, the doctor said it would take a couple of weeks. I'm okay now, but I wish Joe would get here so we can start the therapy. He's on his way pops so relax. Would you go up and get my phone, darling?

Abby picked up Colin's phone and saw he had several text messages. She couldn't resist looking to see who texted. One marked urgent from Jim, one from Auggie and another from that Centry guy GG. What the hell is going on? She didn't dare open them to read, but that didn't mean she didn't want to read them. Abby needed a way to find out why all these people were texting.

Colin took his phone from Abby and noticed all of the messages which he was sure she had to have seen. He gave her a quick look waiting for her to say something. Alright pops, why all the texting? "I suppose they are in response to my inquiries," Colin replied. Were you inquiring about the shooting Colin? Yes and no, some are work-related and updating my company. Okay, so when you find out all of this information, you will share it with your wife, right? I said I would Abby, and I will. In the meantime, can you get Joe, please?

Joe had a key to the house but hardly ever used it. Abby answered the door and conveyed to Joe Colin's current condition. Joe looked worried but told Abby none of these symptoms were unexpected considering. Work your magic, Joe; he's not in a good place. Who would be Abby as you are well aware from personal experience?

Abby left Colin in Joe's hands, and she had to leave to meet Rachel. Dreading going, but she knew there was no sense in putting it off.

Rachel arrived at Ginny's before her mom waiting to hear what was so important that they couldn't meet at home. Only one thing comes to mind, "she didn't want Colin to be there." Shit now worried Rachel thought she would leave and make an excuse later. She stood up to do just that when she saw Abby walking in the door.

Abby kisses Rachel on the forehead, and they sit down, but both seemed uncomfortable. Mom, how's Colin? In pain and agony, Rach but his injuries are healing, and that is all that matters. Glad to hear mom I really am. I wish I could believe that Rachel, I do, but I am not sure I do. God, mom, that's a horrible thing to say, and you can't be serious. Well, I am serious, Rachel, very serious indeed. It has become apparent that you don't like Colin, I don't know why you don't he's done nothing to you to warrant that behavior.

You're being melodramatic mom seriously over the top with your opinions. Don't you talk to me that way, young lady I am not blind to those facts so don't be trying to downplay the situation. Rachel, I did not come here to argue with you. Fine, then why are we here? I wanted to catch up with you see what you're doing. So let's start with college, what are your plans after the end of the year? Are you getting a job for the summer? Are you going to move into the house with Amanda when we move next month? Hold on mom Jesus one question at a time. Why Rach it's the only way to have a conversation with you.

Mom, I am planning on moving into the house, I will get a job. Are those the answers you wanted? It's a start, and now I want to know where you were and what you were doing around the time Colin got shot? What? Why? That is an odd question to ask me. No, I don't believe it is, and you know it. Do I get a chance to answer, or do you think you know what I was doing? I know one thing Rachel; I do not appreciate your attitude. Mom, I was in school studying and or taking exams; you know that, and if not, you should. What I know is that you have become a rude, obstinate person. With that in mind, I want you to know I have made a doctor's appointment for you to get some counseling. It's Obvious; you have issues with your stepfather and your mother. I am not going to therapy, mom. Yes, you will Rachel or suffer the consequences which will consist of no spending money, no car, and you will move back home. What the fuck is going on mom, you have lost your mind. Rachel, you are under twenty-one I am still your guardian you have no choice but to do what I say or have regrets for not doing so.

With that, Rachel got up and left the restaurant.

On her way home, Abby was so heartbroken and sad not only for herself but also for Blake. Abby now knew what Blake told her was, in fact, accurate, and she was feeling bad for treating Blake as if he was the guilty party. Yes, he should have told me voluntarily, but now I realize he was only trying to spare my feelings. Until she figured out what was actually going on, Abby knew she could not tell Colin, but eventually, she would. So much for total disclosure and the no secret pledge.

The burden of her secrets weighed her down.

Colin wanted to return his calls, but he was in so much pain he couldn't focus. Joe suggested he take one of those pain pills and or let him put a morphine patch on his back, Colin choose the later. With pain relief in sight, Colin prioritized his calls. GG first, then Auggie and lastly Jim. He knew the call to Jim would be the longest.

Gabriel and Colin set a time to meet, but not until tomorrow. GG told Colin he had some exciting information to relay when they met. Colin was curious and asked if he could tell him anything now? No, sir, I am still waiting for the final verification of identity. Upon hanging up, Colin was perplexed about that statement.

Auggie and Colin shared information about the upcoming graduation and confirmed a time for the video conference. Auggie filled Colin in on the Otto situation and wanted to get the go-ahead for his arrest and what if any plans to expedite Otto's return to Russia and or imprison him in the states. Colin told Auggie he wanted to speak to Jim about what if any ideas the FBI might have for Otto. *Little did they know was that Nikolai had other plans for Otto.*

Colin rested a bit before calling Jim; he was, after all, recovering from his wounds and needed to pace himself. Again over thinking his and Abby's terrible luck and kept repeating to himself that no matter how difficult it might be, things had to change.

Jim, "sorry about the not calling sooner." No problem Colin, "how are you feeling?" I feel like shit, but life goes on. Jim, any news for me? I do Colin, can you talk freely on this line? Yes, it's a secure line. Colin, I hope you are up to hearing this news and how it came to the surface. I am more than ready to fry someone's ass. Good here goes, I have the CCTV tapes from the TSA, Maxim and I have viewed and reviewed all of them. Maxim? Jim, why the hell is he assisting you on this? Colin, I wanted to keep this information out of the FBI mainstream process. Jim, I trust you and no one else, but if you needed his assistance, then I have to accept your judgment on it. Now, what did you find out? After viewing all the tapes, we did see a person of interest whom we believe is the shooter. Jesus Jim, can you identify this person? Colin, I think, no, I am positive we have identified him. Colin, do you remember the guy who kidnapped Abby from her house; his name is Luke.

Silence......Hello Colin, are you there? Jim, I'm in shock; give me a moment to recover from this distressing news. What the fuck, Jim, are you sure? Yes, confirmed via facial recognition, no doubt about it, it's him. Does anyone else know? Maxim and myself, of course, and the TSA investigator and more than likely the local police. Shit, Jim, I need to go, I need to talk to Abby before she sees this on the news.

Blake was in a full-blown Abby Lynn Wells withdrawal. He was lonely, never being an outgoing personality, he forced himself to go out and try to socialize. Even though he's only been gone a couple of days, he was already homesick, along with being in agony about the past events. Blake knew moving on was his only option. Staring at his old phone, he knew it would be devastating to turn it on for fear there would be no calls from Abby. Putting the phone in his bedside table and then he decided to find a happy hour to visit later in the day. First thing tomorrow, Blake wanted to find a therapist to talk too, a stranger he could speak freely.

Colin found Joe in the kitchen, making some lunch. Joe, "I need to speak with you regarding my call to Jim." Okay but you need to eat, let's talk over lunch, Colin. After Colin finished filling Joe in on Jim's information, Colin asked him if he thought he should tell Abby. Wow is all Joe could think to say. This news is going to be a significant blow to Abby, Colin. Luke was involved in Abby's abduction for Christ's sake, and I would not want her to have to revisit that tragedy. Joe, I am well aware of how she might react to this news, but it's what happened, and I need to tell her before she sees this on the news or someone else tells her.

Colin, remembering his and Abby's promise of not keeping secrets from one another, he knew he had to tell her.

Colin, I am just an outsider looking in. From what I've heard about this guy Luke, does this sound like something he one day decided to do? Hell no, I don't think that at all, as a matter of fact, I'm sure someone set him up and if I had to guess it would be Ed, Abby's ex. Good lord, how's it possible someone like Abby has these fools around her. Joe, it just goes to show you that one doesn't have to be in my line of work to have drama, fear, and idiots making your life hell. Evidently, not Colin.

Chapter 9

Abby drove around, thinking about how to handle the information she had discovered. So much to consider, and what repercussions could happen to her daughter for her part in this action, she so carelessly got involved. Abby knew deep down that Rachel was the instigator of the act. Now crying in her car with no one to console her, Abby was sure she had to confess all to Colin even inviting Blake over to get the information she needed. Surely he would understand all I was trying to do was eliminate suspects one at a time.

Make amends Abby, start with Colin then Blake.

Amanda called her mom, but Colin answered the phone. Hey, dad, what's up and how are you feeling? Awe Amanda, I like the sound of that, I'm doing okay a little tired but recovering none the less. Good to hear, "can I speak with mom?" Abby's not here but should be home soon, can I have her call you sweetie? Yes, please, so it's important. Is something wrong, Amanda? I'm not sure, Colin, but I wanted to talk to mom about Rachel. "What about Rachel, is she alright?" Hell no she's not alright if I didn't know her I would swear she was doing drugs. Amanda, why don't you come over for dinner, in fact, it would be nice if you could cook. Cook, are you joking Colin I don't cook furthermore no one would eat my food?

Please come to dinner if we need to we'll get a carryout. On my way, pops! When Amanda ended the call, Colin thought to himself how much he enjoyed that girl. He was not able to be the father he wanted to be to his daughters and now was his chance to be one to Abby's girls and his soon to be grandchild.

Colin decided to call GG before Amanda arrived. He wanted to see what information, if any, Gabriel had he didn't want to wait any longer. When Gabriel saw Colin's number on his caller ID, he was reluctant to answer. GG always had an intuition of which he depended on to help him unravel his investigations. This was one-time Gabriel hoped he was wrong about the events at Colin's home and the strange man. Gabriel knew this call could be a career changer, but none the less he had to take the call.

Not one to prolong the inevitable GG merely cut to the chase. Mr. Cavanaugh, I thought we were meeting tomorrow? Gabriel, if you have something to say, please do and now. I am not a very patient man these days. Sir, the news I have may or may not be relevant to your misfortune, but I now have the results. Gabriel, please, for god's sake, get to the point.

The evening before your hospital release, your wife had a late-night visitor. And this has what to do with the shooting? Sir, please bear with me. When I say late night, I am talking well after midnight, and he did not leave until 2 a.m. *Now GG had Colin's attention!* GG just so I am clear on your surveillance, "a man went to my home sometime after midnight and left about 2 a.m." Yes, correct, sir. I'm assuming you now know the identity of this person. "I do, sir, his name is Blake Thomason." Colin, all of a sudden, felt ill; he couldn't breathe. He asked GG to hold on a second." Colin ran to the bathroom or maybe hobbled there. He splashed water on his face, and at that moment, he saw his reflection in the mirror, old is what he saw.

GG, do you have any explanation as to why this man visited Abby at such a late hour? I do not, and that's the reason I was reluctant to bring it up. But after rethinking the visit, I thought it might indeed lead somewhere. So this is all you have thus far concerning the shooting? Yes, sir, it is, but I will continue to investigate and keep you informed. No, I do not want you pursuing this any longer, and I do not want you to discuss with anyone the results of the man or his identity. But sir, I have to file a report with my supervisor. Gabriel, no one is more superior than I am. Fine sir, of course, you are correct, I will dispose of the information I have gathered on this assignment. Thanks, Gabriel, and have a good night.

Jesus fucking Christ, it just never ends, and for that matter, it keeps getting worse.

Colin is walking or is that limping around in circles trying to decide how to approach not only the Rachel issue but now that fucking choir boy Blake. Why in the hell did I protect that asshole from being arrested and prosecuted for killing Jaci? What is my wife up too and Abby had better have a reason for anyone being in our home that late?

Amanda arrived within minutes after Colin hung up with Gabriel.

"Colin, you're not looking so good, are you okay," Amanda asked? She immediately hugged Colin but ever so gently. Then she jokingly said. "isn't it time you and mom took a break from your unlucky streak?" Amanda, dear, "nothing would make me happier."

Let's order some food, Abby will be here shortly. Chinese okay with you, Colin? Anything is good with me as long as it's not hospital food. Amanda laughed!

Both Colin and Amanda heard Abby open the door. Colin looked at Amanda, who had a "what the hell," look on her face. Amanda offered to pick up their food and then suggested he should see what's up with Abby. Yep, he said, "that's a good idea." He then handed her his credit card.

Colin hobbles up the stairs, where he finds Abby sitting on the bed, crying. Darling, "what in the world is this about?" Oh, pops, things keep getting worse for us. That might be true darling, but is it worth crying? Colin gets a few tissues and hands one to Abby, and he uses the other one to wipe the tears from her cheeks.

What has happened Abby to cause you to cry? Colin, I need to talk to you, but I can't with Amanda here, its severe pops very serious. Is she coming back? Yes, she went to get our dinner. Now is good, Abby let's get whatever is bothering you out in the open. If Amanda comes back, I will have her eat without us.

Colin proceeds to put his arm around her for comfort, but in reality, he knew the news was going to be disturbing. Start from the beginning, darling, don't leave anything out.

It's about the shooting, Colin. Abby, what could you possibly know about the shooting? I know a lot, Colin, because I have been investigating on my own for some time now. What the fuck are you talking about Abby, he was furious. Now her tears were flowing, and she was almost inconsolable. Jesus Abby, please tell me why the hell you are so upset? Stop crying **now**! Abby tried to get hold of her emotions, but she seemed to be unable to control herself. Colin went to the bathroom and got her a cup of water and a damp washcloth. Here darling, drink this and wipe your face off, the freshwater will feel good. You're not alone, Abby I also have some news about the shooting. What?

Abby jumped off of the bed, startled by this revelation and said, "let's go downstairs pops, I need a drink."

You go first pops, please, what information do you have? Abby, I want you to start, why you wanted to play detective, and second, what did you discover that has you so upset? I'm afraid Colin, the information I have found this not only disturbing, but it leaves me so sad I can't even function.

Abby, please, I am begging you to tell me what is bothering you. Darling, you know I will understand and support whatever it is. Fine, I'll start from the beginning....

When you were in the hospital lying there looking so horrible, it reminded me of how you must have felt when it was me in the same situation. I knew then that I wanted to do what you and Jim did. Find the shooter and bring them to justice. Colin rolls his eyes in disbelief. Pops don't make fun of me; I am a competent woman, and you know that. I wasn't darling, but I am still waiting for you to tell me what you know. Please, Abby!

I started with a list of suspects I thought could have had a reason for hurting you. I decided to approach the investigation from an elimination process. Don't be mad, but I started with Blake. With that com-

ment, Colin stood up and threw his hands in the air. What the hell is wrong with you pops? Nothing, please go on Abby. I had a plan I started with him, and I called him on the night before you came home asking him to please come over I wanted to talk with him. Blake said he would come by later, but I fell asleep, so I guess he left anyway he called me about midnight and said he was at the back door. I got up and went down to let him in.

That's somewhat late for visiting, isn't it Abby? Of course, it is Colin, but I had a plan, and I wanted to keep it going. Continue, please, Abby. When he came in, I told him what I wanted. And if he knew of anyone that might want to harm you. To say the least, Colin he was shocked that I might suspect him. But the strange thing was, his behavior was out of the ordinary for him, he was nervous and anxious, so I started to sense he did know something. I offered him a glass of wine, and then I acted as I did suspect him. But he had no idea that I didn't know crap.

So, darling, did you need to seduce him to get the information? What the hell are you talking about pops? I asked you a question Abby, did you come on to him to get the information, it's a simple question. You're an asswipe Colin, no, I did no such thing because I'm smarter than that. I let him believe I already knew." I see," Colin said. Abby could tell he didn't believe her for one minute, but she continued the story. I told Blake I knew what had happened, so I wanted his version of the story before I went to the police. That's all it took, and then he told me what he knew. That was when Abby lost it again, crying uncontrollably. Stop it, Abby, right fucking now. What the hell did he tell you? Oh, pops, it is so horrible, and I am so sorry. Colin had had enough and told Abby to please spit it out.

It was Rachel pops; it was my flesh and blood. Rachel, Abby, that's ridiculous why would he tell you something so cruel. Because she told him the shooting was her idea, but she only wanted to scare you and never intended for you to get shot.

Now Colin was all ears and wondered if it was time to come clean with his wife on his information.

Abby, is that all? No, pops, I met Rachel for breakfast this morning, and I asked her about the information I got from Blake. The horrible thing is, she never flinched or denied it. She told me she went to visit her father, and they discussed a plan. Somehow they got Luke involved, and I suppose he was the one that shot you. Rachel said she was surprised at how fast Ed jumped on the opportunity to get even with you.

Tears, tears, and more tears!

I am afraid for my daughter Colin; she has involved herself in a criminal situation. I don't know what to do. Stop crying, Abby. I also have some information. I only found out myself a couple of hours ago that the shooter was Luke; they have him on CCTV, darling he is busted. So this whole time, you knew it was him, and you just let me rant on like you didn't know. Yes, I did Abby, but I sure as hell didn't think you would tell me it was Rachel's idea. What was the purpose of my spilling my guts then? What's going on, Colin? Shit, Abby, my investigator, he saw Blake enter the house. I was going to ask you about it later. I had no idea it was related to your information.

Wow pops, you wanted to hear what I had to say before you told me your news. Isn't that nice of you, Colin, and what pray tell did you think he was doing here that late? Okay, Abby let's not let this get out of hand, I didn't imagine anything sinister. I just found out by accident and was going to tell you later. Again I had no idea he was involved in this business until you told me. To be clear pops, Blake had nothing to do with the shooting, Rachel likes Blake, it seems she told him when she had too much to drink.

Why was your daughter having drinks with your friend Abby? I have no idea Colin; we should ask her if the opportunity arises.

Good now, Abby, are we both on the same page with what happened? Colin, did you think Blake was here for some other reason? No darling I did not, other than it was late, so I merely was going to ask you why he was visiting at that hour. Colin had a gut feeling regarding Blake, and it never goes away! Okay, then let's move on and see how we can keep Rachel out of jail.

Chapter 10

Maxim despised answering to Jim, especially when the subject involves Mr. Colin Cavanaugh, who happens to be married to the most amazing woman in the world. Ask me if I care who attempted to shoot his ass, ask me if I care that he didn't die because I don't. Мне, блядь, все равно! (*I fucking do not care!*)

Jim summons Maxim into his office for a quick meeting, oh, and of course, it involves the main man who had become the topic of much discussion of late. Maxim, "please have a seat, I want to fill you in on the investigation into Colin's shooter." I was in the middle of a report, Jim, but I can spare a few minutes. What the hell is up with you, Max? I'm fine, Jim, what is the latest on the shooting? The shooter identified as one Luke Hamilton, and law enforcement is after him as we speak. The guy is an idiot and didn't bother to see if the area had cameras, obviously an amateur. Jim, stop let me guess how this went down; the shooting was personal, the shooter was someone who knew Mr. Cavanaugh. And he also knows his wife, am I right on target or what? Well, Max, how bright you are and right of course, unfortunately, the bureau could not assume the attempt was personal; that's why we investigated. Are we done here, Jim?

No, we are not fucking done!

Max, you're going back to Costa Rica for an undercover operation involving a couple of foreign agents suspected of attempting to infiltrate the training camp.

You are not serious! (Ты несерьезно!) Hey, asshole no Russian spoken here, understand. Maxim is in the panic mode now; he has suspected that that is where Nikolai is hanging out. Could my life be any more fucked up?

Here's the assignment packet, your first stop is to see Colin who will review the details before leaving for Costa Rica. Jim, this is not a good plan, these recruits know me, and they know I have turned. Tell me you aren't concerned about that small detail. It's a slight concern, but only if they see you, you, of course, will be incognito out of sight. Undercover Maxim. Read the assignment, and then you will be clear on what we hope to accomplish. If not, Colin will make it very clear.

Maxim left the meeting more pissed off than when he went in. Once home, he immediately got his secure phone and sent Nikolai a coded message marking it urgent. How in the hell am I going to apprehend one of our Russian operatives? So many questions could Nikolai actually be in Costa Rica, and if so, why? I have suspected for a while now that he was operating in that area of Central America, but to what end I am not sure.

The only good thing to come out of that meeting was, Abby, he was going to have an opportunity to see her again. And for that, he was eternally grateful for the asshole Jim. Maxim was well aware of the caution he must adhere too when in The Snowman's presence. Even though Maxim knew Colin was recovering from his wounds, he wasn't a man one could take lightly. Maxim decided to review his dossier on Colin if only to remind himself that he could not underestimate the man. Not expecting a return text anytime soon, he decided to get some dinner and possibly visit the local neighborhood bar for a few drinks. Life in America is the most boring assignment Maxim has ever endured. But allowing The Snowman to catch him and turn him might be one of his most personal achievements ever. Leading, of course, to the woman he has come to love and want. To think that Colin and the FBI thought they apprehended a Russian spy by chance is very laughable indeed.

Rachel was in the waiting area at the prison provided for visiting family, appalled by the entire facility she tried to focus on her reasons for visiting her father. Yes, he was not ever getting an award for "father of the year," nor has he ever done anything positive in his recent life, but he was her dad. He used to be a very upstanding and honorable person with a thriving business. Mom certainly would have never married him otherwise.

The people waiting in the room with her didn't appear to be upstanding citizens of any type. Shabbily dressed along with little kids hanging on them, waiting their turn to visit their criminal family member. Gross was the only word Rachel could think of, but here she was sitting in the same gross room in the same hellhole called prison life waiting to see her criminal father.

Some touch of regret-filled Rachel in the pit of her stomach. Even though she was the ringleader in this debacle, she never intended for Luke to harm or hurt Colin. Frightening him was the plan not shooting his ass, and for that, she blamed her father. Hoping to get some information from him was her purpose in being here, along with alerting him that everyone knew Luke was the shooter.

The guard summoned Rachel to the sign-in register process area, from there she was led to an area of small desks, and there he was behind the glass with a phone so that he could communicate. *Jesus, I hate this!*

Rachel, I'm pleasantly surprised to see you came to visit. Dad, this is not a visit I think you're going to like. "Why is that sweetie?" Mom knows I was involved, and right off, she suspected you were involved as well. How the hell did she figure that out, Rach? It's my fault, dad I went to happy hour with Blake and had too much to drink. I blurted it out of my mouth, I think, and as soon as I said it, I regretted doing so. Jesus Rachel, this opens you up to what could lead to your being a shit load of trouble. I know dad. I'm well aware of that. Mom was furious with me, and that asshole of a husband of hers; I am sure knows by now.

Rachel, did Blake tell your mother? Of course, he did dad because I didn't. But dad, all of this is Luke's fault he was only supposed to scare Colin not really shoot him. What's done is done Rach there is no going back, I think Luke wanted to kill that guy because he thought it would make amends for him testifying against me. Dad, I am not in the mom and Colin loop, but from what I understand, Colin is not a person you want to be on the wrong side. I think he is some black ops guy or an assassin. Oh, for God's sake, Rachel, that is ridiculous. No, I don't think so dad, how did he manage to find mom and rescue her from that kidnapping debacle. Haven't you ever thought about that? You have some valid points, Rach, I need to think this over

In the meantime, Rachel, you need to stay away from home until I can come up with some plan to keep you out of trouble. I will call you as soon as I have an idea in place. Oh, dad, I am so worried not only for me but for you and Luke. Calm down and stay out of sight for the time being. Dad, I have to go to school the year is ending, and I have exams, crap and Amanda's graduation is in a few weeks, this is horrible, and I hate myself for being such an ass. With that, she turned and left.

Walking to her car, Rachel thought she would never revisit this place even if it meant not seeing her father. Regrets ravished her insides; as a father, he should have tried to stop her crazy idea. Not make it fit his agenda. I'm such an idiot and a horrible example of a daughter. On her drive home, she decided to come clean with Colin, get this over with, make amends to him and mom. Reflecting on why mom was so in love with him still haunted Rachel, but the least she thought she could do was give the man the benefit of the doubt. Possibly there was something he could do to help keep me out of trouble. Even if that was a doable thing, there was Luke to worry about, and he inevitably would spill the beans, blaming me for it all.

Amanda returned with dinner and apologized for taking so long due to the restaurant stating that there was a backup. Abby and Colin both looked at each other rolling their eyes and then started laughing. What's so funny? "Nothing, sweetie, nothing at all," Colin says. Time to eat Abby, I'm starving. What's new pops, you're always hungry and ready to eat.

Amanda observed her mother, and at once, she knew something was amiss, and she looks like she had been crying. Colin appeared to be overly attentive even though he was the one in need of attending too. *What the hell had happened here?*

As soon as Amanda left, Colin realized how bad his back was hurting. He suggested they both get some rest, read or watch television in bed. It was early, but the day turned out to be more stressful than either one of them needed. Abby agreed but told Colin that she might sleep in the spare room. Why darling would you do that? I feel we need a break. All of this drama has me very depressed, starting with losing our baby to your shooting and up to Rachels's behavior. I cannot take any more trauma Colin it has worn me out. Please don't stay in that room, Abby. I need you now more than ever.

Colin, I feel out of sorts lately, maybe I need to see my doctor again or the therapist. That might be a good idea, Abby, but for now, please stay with me tonight. I love you, darling, and I want us to be united in our efforts to make things less complicated. Abby, I want us to move into our new home as soon as possible. I believe it will take our minds off of all things tragic. Start fresh, what do you think, darling? I will call the builder tomorrow and see how much longer he needs to finish.

Abby, I won't let anything happen to Rachel, I know she is not a fan of mine, but she is your daughter. I have a plan not only to fry Ed's ass, but I believe I can find Luke before he is arrested and talk him into keeping Rachel out of harm's way. Can you really pull that off pops? Yes, I believe I can, Jim will be in town tomorrow with Maxim. I have a meeting with them. Colin, why is Jim bringing that Russian to see you? Business Abby, what else. Is it a secret, Colin? Of course, it is darling, and its nothing you need to worry about, business plans for an undercover assignment.

Abby was delighted and worried about the possibility of seeing Maxim, but it would most certainly take her mind off her current woes. Would he be excited to see me? Yes, I believe he would be, but the question is, am I ready to walk toward the edge of that cliff again? I so often -think there will be a point where I will fall off.

Abby left the bathroom refreshed and ready to relax with her unfinished novel. Colin turned on the television. Channel surfing irritated Abby to no end. Pops for goodness sake, please find something to watch. Darling, I'm feeling much better how about a hug from my beautiful wife? First, a hug then a few kisses and then well, you know where hugs and kisses lead pops. I do indeed darling, so what do you think? I think your back isn't ready for much more than a few kisses and hugs. Oh, Abby, you're such a spoilsport. No, I'm trying to make sure you heal correctly, and quickly then you can have all the kisses you want.

Chapter 11

Abby and Colin were having coffee in the kitchen when they heard someone coming in the front door. Colin, ever the worrier, got up to see who had not even knocked on the door before entering. Abby said, "pops, it can only be someone with a key, so relax already." Ha, Colin replies, "famous last words, my dear."

Rachel yells out, "mom; it's me." We're in the kitchen Rach, come on in, please. Colin rolls his eyes as if not saying to her, "you were right."

What brings you out so early and on a school day? I wanted to speak with mom and you, Colin. Okay, Rachel, what's on your mind? I want to tell both of you all of the facts leading up to the unplanned shooting of Colin. I must come clean with it all mom, and I will start with, "I am so sorry that he shot you, Colin, I really am." Okay, Rachel said Colin, "let's hear what you have to say, and then we will go from there."

After Rachel spilled her guts about what happened, Colin thought the whole thing more outlandish than he did before. Abby, on the other hand, found the facts not only unimaginable, but her daughter's part was heartbreaking.

Then Rachel breaks this news.......

I went to visit Dad at the prison yesterday. "Why the fuck did you do that," Colin said? I wanted to tell him Blake told mom, but I didn't tell him anything about Luke or how it came to be that Luke shot Colin. I wanted to know if dad gave that order. Mom, Colin, the plan I swear was to only scare you not for you to get shot. None of that was my idea, and for that, I am so sorry. Well, Rachel, what the hell did Ed say about the change of plans? Did he tell Luke to shoot to kill or not? Yes, Colin, he did, and he confessed to me that until you were dead, he would keep trying. Abby was now on her feet, pacing back and forth with worry for Rachel and what could happen to her.

Colin got up and left the room, Abby ran after him, but he put his hand up and said, "I need a moment to think and to control my urge to kill your mother fucking ex-husband Abby." These idiots don't have any idea who they're dealing with Abby. I get it pops, but don't think for one minute you're leaving me out of this mess; when you figure out what you're going to do, I want to know. You have my word, darling; you will be the first to know.

Fighting an international gang of ISIS members was easier than dealing with family drama of which I never thought possible. Colin sat down in the bedroom, going over in his head how the hell is he going to get a handle on his life. The situation Rachel has gotten herself in was severe, and if it ever came out that she was the instigator of it, she was going to jail. Even though he hated the thought of asking Jim for help, Colin knew that was the only way of keeping Rachel safe. Thank god Jim would be available later in the day for the meeting.

Colin returned to find Abby and Rachel in the living room. They both looked as if the world was about to end. Ladies, I have decided that number one Rachel's involvement in this debacle will never come to the surface. Number two, I am going to go to whatever lengths necessary to make sure Ed Wells never leaves prison. The two of you need to listen to me and follow my instructions. Rachel, you are never to discuss with anyone your involvement, especially Amanda. Abby, I need you to do the same, and this is a hard thing for me to say, but I need you to call Blake and convince him of the same thing. Can you both do what I asked? Rachel happily agreed. Abby looked concerned, and Colin asked her if calling was a problem? I can try to call, but he's out of the country. I think Blake is in Spain, that's where his family lives. It's critical Abby that you speak with him; he cannot tell another soul about this, understand. I do pops, and I will find a way to get in touch with him.

Abby asked Rachel if she wanted some breakfast, no thanks mom I have to get to class before I'm late. Colin told her not to worry that everything would work out; he would see that it did.

Colin excused himself to prepare for his meeting. Abby said she was going to research what time zone Spain was in so she could try to reach Blake.

Jim filled Maxim in on the assignment before their meeting with Colin and Joe. Maxim was in dire need of that return text from Nikolai and was quite worried as to why he had not responded thus far. Time was running out on giving Nikolai the heads up on his new assignment.

Maxim thought this seemed like an assassination of a rookie agent in training, why he was being sent did not make sense. His biggest fear was running into other recruits that would recognize him. Incognito was especially important.

Colin, Joe, along with Jim and Maxim, met at the local office. Joe assured them that the office was free of any bugs. Colin smiled and was pleased that Joe had progressed in his position at such a fast pace. Not ready for field duty but none the less a considerable help to Colin. Jim outlined Maxim's assignment and expressed to him that this was an out of jurisdiction assignment for Centry Security International, not the FBI. Maxim looked surprised and nearly started to speak out of turn until Jim held up his hand in objection before Max could speak.

Colin threw his car keys to Maxim and asked him if he could find his way to Abby's house. Why would I want to go to your home, Mr. Cavanaugh? Because I need to have a private meeting with Jim and Joe, that's why. To be clear, Maxim do not ever question my instructions again, or you and I will have issues understood? Oh, I do understand what you said, sir, but what you need to know is I don't work for you, *understand*? Fuming Colin replied, "get the fuck out of here now before I forget I'm injured." Easy boys, we're all on the same team here. With that, Maxim happily headed for Abby's, how lucky can a guy get? Well, what I should have said is, "non-professional behavior on both ends." Shut the hell up, Jim; I couldn't dislike anyone more than that killer! What is it you want to talk about Colin?

Abby just had a long bath and was relaxing by the fireplace when Maxim rang the doorbell. When Abby opened the door and saw him standing there staring at her, she almost fainted, she must have looked a mess. Good lord Maxim, please come in, sorry about my attire I just got out of the shower. "Beautiful is the first word I can think of Abby," and you look so shall I say, fresh and bare. Anyone home Abby? No why? With that, he pulled off the robe she had on, and it was the only thing she had on.

Maxim, that was foolish. No, I think not, because I know where your husband is, so it's just us. He started to pull her close, she reached for her robe, but he got to it first. Oh no, you don't. I've waited a long time to see you. Maxim, this is not the place if Colin comes home, he will kill you. Stop worrying Abby and come closer please I have missed you so much, I want you and now. Abby came close to him, putting her hands inside his suit coat, moving them down the front of his trousers until she reached what she wanted. Oh my god, Abby, don't start something we can't finish.

As they kissed with so much passion and desire, Abby whispered in his ear that she wanted him and badly, but now was not the time. Before the words were out of her mouth, he forced her against the wall. She could no longer fight him off, and she didn't want too. While being in an uncontrolled heightened state of sexual arousal, Abby knew this was wrong, but she was helpless in this state of passion. So much for having control of my desires for this man.

Jesus Maxim control yourself and get dressed; now, I need to get dressed before they get here. Tell me, Abby, you liked, right? Abby laughed at his bad language and accent, but she knew he needed to hear that she was sexually attracted. Yes, Maxim, I liked it, but I would have liked our lovemaking to be somewhere else and for a more extended time. How long will you be here, Maxim? I wish I knew, but I believe when Jim gets here, they will let me know. Well, when they do, let me know, and if possible, I want to meet. Oh, Abby, you can count on that.

As Abby stood in the shower with cold water flowing down her body, she was in disbelief of what had transpired. Was she dreaming, or did that handsome hunk rape her in her own home? Rape was not what happened; Abby knew as soon as she saw him, something unreal was going to happen. Abby thought about her pledge to herself that she would not be bad any longer. That she would be faithful to Colin, and most of all, that she would not have sex in their home. *Shit, so much for pledges!*

Jim was very interested as to why Colin wanted him to stay back for another meeting. All Jim could think of was, "what has Abby done now."

Colin and Joe had Jim's undivided attention now that the Russian asshole was gone. Colin wasn't amused by Jim's decision to send Maxim back to Costa Rica; in a way, it was a step backward for someone like Maxim. Earth to Colin, what do you want, and how can I help with whatever your beautiful wife has gotten into now? Oh, very funny, Jim, but I am happy to say it's not my wife this time. Colin gave Jim the entire chain of events up to and including this morning's confession from Rachel.

It never ends with you, Colin, I must say your personal life isn't dull. Okay, Jim, I get it, but the question is, can you offer any solution to the problem or not? Has any law enforcement agency picked up Luke yet? Not that I am aware, but I would bet he's hiding out somewhere. All right, I suggest we find him before they do, we can have a little chat about him placing blame on Ed, and he was following orders. Jim, the guy, is an idiot, and I swear he would hurt his own mother for a dime. We could merely have the guy disappear if you wanted Colin. I would love nothing more, but let's find him then decide his fate. I'm not convinced that Luke will keep his mouth shut forever, so once we have him, he will need to convince us otherwise.

Abby asked Maxim if he wanted something to eat and some coffee. You American's don't know how to make coffee, let me make some for you. Abby, what do you think the three of them are discussing? Maxim, I believe it has to do with my daughter, Rachel. What about her, Abby? If there is a problem, can I help? Abby thought long and hard about going any further with this conversation. Let me tell you what I know, Maxim, and then you tell me if you can help my little girl. When Abby finished talking, Maxim told Abby that he would take care of the problem and for her not to worry, consider it done.

Abby provided Maxim with all the information he needed. She was unsure it was wise to get Maxim involved, but too late now, and he would take care of the problem of that she was sure.

Colin called Abby and asked if Maxim was still there and if so, would they please meet him and Jim at The Chateau for dinner. Abby replied, "of course, pops, but why in the world is this man here without you?" I will explain later Abby it was unavoidable. What time do you want us to meet? Leave the house about five we will already be there in the lounge. Thanks, Colin, I love driving around with a known assassin. Don't be an ass darling; we couldn't exactly have him roaming around the neighborhood could we now. Oh, of course not pops, but it's okay to leave him alone with your wife. There you go again being an ass! She hung up!

Maxim help yourself to a cocktail I need to get dressed for dinner it appears we're all going out. Can I help you dress, Abby? Hell no, stay where you are before you sign our death warrants.

Waiting for a woman to dress is as good as any excuse to drink, so Maxim helped himself to the Cavanaugh bar. And a well-stocked bar indeed he thought, wonder who drinks all of this very American liqueur? His phone buzzed, and he was delighted to see Nikolai's code pop up. Feeling it was secure to answer it since Abby was upstairs and out of earshot. Maxim returned the proper code for secure connections, and then Nikolai answered.

Comrade, so good to hear from you. What's up, Max? I wanted to alert you regarding my next assignment; I am going to Costa Rica; the order is to eliminate one Otto Zimmerman. Allegedly he is a threat to the Americans and not the FBI. Max, what the hell does that mean, not the FBI, isn't that who you're working for? It's a covert operation ran by and for the benefit of Centry Security International, Colin Cavanaugh's company. Maxim, this is not good news, you need to stop this plan. Max, do you hear me you must find a way to void this assignment. Hello Max!!! What the fuck happened.

As soon as Maxim heard Abby coming down the stairs, he hung up and without any goodbyes. Shit, I need some privacy and as quickly as possible.

While going into the spare bedroom for a dress she had in the closet, Abby heard Maxim talking on the phone, who the hell was he talking too? She listened for a minute and then was in disbelief of what she heard. About to head downstairs, she was shaking a bit, Abby knew she had to act as normal as possible until she could get Colin by himself to alert him about Maxim's phone call.

As Abby entered the foyer, she did a turnaround showing off her rather skimpy dress. Well, Maxim, will this do? Come closer, and I will tell you if I like it or not. Oh, I'm not sure that's a good idea for the second time today, Maxim. Let me decide, Abby, my love. Abby moves closer and closer, teasing him, her dress was way off base for a weeknight dinner, and she knew it was. Oh God Abby, you make me a crazy Russian; I want to make love to you please tell me we can get together before I leave? Well, that is up to you; you're the one going, not me, so let me know. Oh, you can depend on that. We need to leave Maxim, and I'll drive.

When Abby and Maxim entered the restaurant heads turned, she looked like a movie star, and she knew it. Colin stared at his wife and wondered why she overdressed for dinner? Even though he loved how she looked, he didn't appreciate all the men in the room staring at her.

Whispering in his wife's ear, Colin says. "you look beautiful darling I love the dress, is it new?" Yes, I just haven't had an occasion to wear it. I bought it in Paris pops it was expensive, remember? Oh, I do so remember that very pricey shopping excursion in a moment of anger. Jim merely shook his head and again was reminded why his friend would do anything for this woman. Could I blame him, not in a million years? Jim bought drinks all around as they waited to be seated. So Abby, when will that mansion be ready to move? Our walkthrough is in two days, and we are so excited, right, honey? *Honey, what the hell is that?*

Something is off-center; Colin sensed it from the moment Abby walked in. The dress and calling me honey, then she ordered a Manhattan for a cocktail. This is not my wife. Somehow I need to get her aside to talk, but I fear if it has something to do with Jim or Maxim, they may suspect something. Am I overly cautious hell yes I am? Letting it go, for now, Colin knew when dinner was over, Jim will take Maxim with him.

Dinner was divine, but watching Abby order food she never ate was just another tip for me, and I was getting more anxious as the evening went along. Maxim ordered an after-dinner drink, a White Russian, perfect he announced. Jim asked why I wasn't drinking, and I reminded him that I was still taking prescription medications. Then I said that I was tired and needed to go home. About then, Maxim asked Jim when they were heading out of town? Jim replied that the final arrangements were being made, but he thought they would leave for the airport day after tomorrow. Maxim was sure Abby heard as well, and with that, he excused himself to the men's room. Well, goodnight Abby and I are leaving; maybe we'll see you before you go.

Abby gave Jim a peck on his cheek, and he returned the same. She, in turn, handed Colin the valet ticket and headed for the ladies' room. As she entered the restroom, Maxim came out of the men's. Love did you hear I will be here for another day and a half. Please text when we can be together? I will Maxim, but keep in mind Colin is home recovering, so it will be harder to merely leave, but I will think of some way to make it happen.

Chapter 12

As soon as the valet returned their car, Colin got in the driver's seat because Abby was just a bit drunk. He only waited until he pulled out into the main street before practically yelling for Abby to tell him what the fuck was going on. Pops are we out of range now because I think I am going to throw up if I don't talk to you and soon. Colin, you need to pull over somewhere out of sight and stop so I can speak to you. What the hell Abby can't it wait until we get home, which I might add is like in a few minutes. No, for God's sake, Colin, I want to talk now and not in the house what if its bugged? The park Colin head to the park, please hurry.

What in the name of God could be so important that she doesn't want to talk in our house?

Okay, Abby, I'm stopped, and I'm ready to hear whatever it is you want to tell me, but I'm hoping you're not asking for a divorce? What are you crazy pops, this is serious? Start from the beginning, Abby.

So to start, I was not happy at all that you sent that crazy Russian for me to entertain. But had you not done that, I would not have discovered that he is a double agent. Colin's eye's bulged out, and his mouth dropped in utter amazement. Abby darling Maxim is not a double agent he is although a prior Russian spy who now works for the FBI as a spy, you knew that. Colin, you and Jim are delusional if you believe that because after I heard Maxim on the phone, there is no doubt he's a double agent. What the fuck are you talking about, Abby?

Shit Abby start from the beginning and don't leave out a word I need to evaluate and try to absorb what you're saying. Fine, after you called, I told Maxim to fix himself a drink while I went upstairs to get dressed. I wanted to wear something special more to make Jim jealous than for you. God, Abby, what the hell? I don't like Jim pops, so I wanted him to know what you have, and he doesn't. Sorry, it was childish. Please, Abby, go on. So anyway, the dress was in the spare bedroom closet I only had on my underwear, so I quietly walked to the hallway when I heard him on the phone.

And?

As soon as I heard the words, "Nikolai, I'm heading to Costa Rica." I knew that the person Maxim was talking with was Russian. Then he told this Nikolai guy he was being sent to assassinate a man named Otto Zimmerman, and that he was pissed because it was an assignment beneath his talents, and he was insulted. He did mention that the job was not for the FBI but Centry Security; that's when I left to get my dress. Colin, I was scared to death.

Colin was beyond worried that Abby was correct, was it possible that this asshole could fool Jim and myself? How is he communicating without being found out, is Jim still doing surveillance on him like they always do on new agents? Colin tried to calm Abby, but it was to no avail. Darling let's go home and get ready for bed, I have a way to contact Jim without Maxim finding out so don't worry about that. What is going on, Colin? Darling, as soon as I find out, I will tell you, but if that is all you heard, he could have been talking with a friend. Oversharing and against the rules, hell yes, but that alone doesn't make him a double agent. Now, how about a shower with my wife, whom I miss so much. Pops, are you kidding how you can think about sex at a time like this? Abby, I understand why you reacted as you did, but believe me, there is more to this story. Leave it to me to find out the details, as you know, "the devils in the details," my darling. Now about that shower.

Colin knew making love lying down in bed was not a good idea just yet, but standing up was an option. When he entered the shower and saw his wife naked and the hot water rolling off her perfect body, he knew no matter how much it hurt; he was all in. Abby sensed his need for closeness, so she started to lather up his body with the most fantastic massage. Oh my darling, it has been too long. I have missed you so much. Colin moved Abby to the shower wall, and from there, it was only pure passion and ecstasy. The funny thing was he did not feel any pain, and for that, he was grateful.

Maxim couldn't even think about sleeping; he had so much on his mind. First, he needed to find this guy Luke; he thought he knew how. With the information, Abby gave him he tried the local white pages for a telephone number but nothing there. He went online to find a "people search program." Sure enough, there he was Maxim did a reverse search so he could get an address. Damn that was too easy now he needed a car, he knew there was a car rental agency working from the hotel lobby, so he headed for it. Hoping Jim was in his room and not out and about Maxim left.

With the address in his secure phone, Maxim headed to Luke's house. It was only a twenty-minute drive using the GPS app; when he reached the house, Maxim parked down the street and waited. The house was dark, but Maxim was sure Luke was in there hiding from the police. He decided to see if there was a street behind the house, and he would enter from the rear. Looking around for cameras was critical; he couldn't chance being caught here. Driving around the area proved to be a good idea; there was a park behind his house surrounded by woods. He entered the park but chose to park outside away from the lights in the parking lot.

Maxim pulled his hoodie up over his head and walked the few blocks to the house via the park. Once he found the house, he jumped over the fence surrounding it and again looked for any recording devices. From what he had heard about this guy, he wasn't too smart, so Maxim didn't expect any methods of detection in place. Good news on that front. He quickly entered the house via a basement door. This guy is an idiot! It was very dark but had just enough moonlight shining through the window for him to see the stairs. Creeping ever so softly, he finds a door which crazy as seems was open. Still, he saw no lights on; he had a penlight on his keychain, so he used that for better vision.

No one on the first floor, which meant he was upstairs hiding somewhere. Again Maxim used the dim light to find stairs; he climbed them one at a time, making sure there were no squeaks or noise. The home appeared to be a three-bedroom home, but once he was upstairs, he could hear what he thought was a television. All lights were out, but under a door, there was a slight ray of light coming from underneath. Maxim's only worry was if Luke was alone? Abby told him, Luke, never married and had no kids, so he assumed he was alone. He was in front of the door and deciding how best to enter the room when he thought he knew how. Knocking on the door hard and yelling. "come out; this is the police!" To his amazement, Luke opened the door with his hands up. A very shocked Luke says, "Who the hell are you, asshole?"

With the silencer on the weapon, Maxim thought this to be the most effortless kill he ever completed. No chance of leaving behind any evidence, no prints, no bullet casings, no nothing. Now I need to get the hell out of here.

Maxim erased his GPS data, then returned to the rental car counter with the keys, then headed to his room. He thanked the agent and said how much he enjoyed his dinner out. The agent said, "I'm so glad, Mrs. Fieldstone, you have a nice evening now."

And that was that!

Abby and Colin slept in way too long for Colin's liking. His phone started ringing a few hours ago, Joe then Jim and for the grace of god Amanda? What the hell is going on? He called Amanda first, but before she could answer, Abby yelled for him to get downstairs. What a way to start the day. Darling, what is wrong, I'm trying to return Amanda's call. Pops I'm on the phone with her turn on the TV, it seems Luke is dead. Shocked Colin said, "are you fucking kidding me?"

They both were watching the TV when Joe knocked on their door. Colin, "how're things going so far today?" Just peachy! Come on in Joe; we're watching all of the excitement, especially the "supposed" suicide. I know Colin I saw it, what's your take on this? Not a suicide I can tell you that but who did the deed, I have no idea. Abby was trying to contact Rachel, but Amanda said she had exams this morning, and she doesn't take her phone. Amanda offered to go to her classroom and wait for her to finish. They didn't want her to find out by any other means.

Jim and Maxim showed up at the house about an hour later. Jim didn't seem to care one way or the other about Luke nor who killed him. He makes that clear to Colin and Abby. As far as Jim was concerned, the case, according to the TSI and local police, was a suicide. Colin didn't buy that for one minute, but who was he to dispute what ended up being an end to Rachel's nightmare. Abby asks Colin if he thought she still needed to reach Blake. Yes, darling, I think you should tell him to please never mention to anyone what Rachel told him then break the news about Luke.

Abby hated how all of this ended, she would have preferred that someone talk some sense into Luke, but that doesn't matter any longer. Just another tragedy to get over. Abby felt forced to go forward with her life regardless, forced to forget, forced to accept all of this shit since she met her husband. Abby knew at some point she would have decisions to make, possibly the hardest of her life. But that was for another time, for now, she was going forward with her plans, all good and positive intentions. Moving into their new home, Amanda's graduation, Amy's wedding. All of the upcoming events that would put a smile on her face. She no longer wanted to be involved with anything or anyone affiliated with Colin's private business, which includes Jim and Joe and especially Maxim. She knew Maxim was the one that killed Luke; he said he would, and he did. Grateful maybe, afraid of him, hell yes? Would all of these events change her baby girl? Only time would tell Abby thought there was a chance that Rachel would grow up and become the woman Abby wanted her to be.

Maxim was so quiet that even Jim thought it weird. Colin asked Abby if she would get Maxim to go into the kitchen for coffee, so he and Jim could talk freely. Abby rolled her eyes and gave him a look that said, "you are the biggest asswipe ever."

Hey, Maxim how about some of that famous coffee you make? Oh, sure, Mrs. Cavanaugh, I can do that. When they got to the kitchen, Maxim was not volunteering any information about Luke. Abby didn't know if she should bring it up or not. She decided to wait, let him tell her when he was ready. Maxim wanted so badly to tell Abby that he saved her daughter, but with the others in the house, it could wait. He thought she knew anyway, and that pleased him. However, he would remind her that he would be in town tonight and would she meet him at the same hotel at nine this evening.

Colin motioned for Jim to follow him; Jim followed Colin to his office in the lower level of the house. The room was secure, so they both could speak freely.

What's going on Colin, is it necessary to meet down here? Jesus Jim, if it weren't, we wouldn't be down here. Colin went on the tell Jim everything Abby told him last night. To say Jim was stunned with this news would be an understatement. Your thoughts about this, Jim? Obviously, no matter the reason for that call, he violated the bureau's policies. I've heard that name before, so if my memory is correct, Colin, Nikolai is a KGB agent, a Russian spy, and I believe he is of the same level of expertise as Maxim. Meaning Jim, he's an assassin as well? Exactly!

I believe Jim this Nikolai is the same man we saw in a photo taken in Costa Rica a couple of weeks ago. Auggie has the scoop on that incident. I will get with tomorrow.

Why in the hell would Maxim be talking with and passing along his assignment information to this man? Is it possible this man is merely a friend? You can't take that chance, Jim. If I were you, I would speak with Marilyn as soon as possible to see if there is any current intel on this man. And I'm wondering if this Nikolai might currently be in Costa Rica. If this turns out that Maxim is indeed a double agent, you and I are in some deep shit. No, not me, Jim, you, if you remember, I wanted to shoot his ass and be done with him, but you insisted you could turn him. Oh, thanks for that reminder, Colin. The bottom line is I need to move quickly on this mess; Maxim and I leave tomorrow.

Once upstairs, Jim told Maxim he needed to go to the office for some paperwork. Maxim asked what he was supposed to do in the meantime? Go back to your hotel stay there to eat lunch or whatever until I call you, then we will meet for the final details of your assignment. How am I to get to the hotel Jim and how long will you be gone? Take the rental car. Joe will take me to the office. I think it will be later this afternoon. Jim tosses Maxim the keys. Colin tells Abby he needs to work downstairs in his office for a few hours so he can try to find out what is going on with Maxim and this Nikolai person of interest. That's fine pops I have some shopping to do, and I think I will meet Amy and have lunch I miss seeing my friends. Good idea, darling, have a good time.

Abby was barely out of the driveway when she got the text from Maxim, "meet me at the hotel bar, you know where now would be great." Abby knew she had at least a few hours before she had to be home. Her worry was as usual, "in reality, do I want to meet this, man?" There is so much about him I love, his looks, a great lover, but he reeks of mystery and intrigue which scares the hell out of me. Knowing he kills for a living should be reason enough to stay the hell away. But I knew I couldn't; I wanted to see him, and I wanted Maxim in every sense.

Abby entered the hotel from the back entrance, which allowed her to get to the lounge without being seen. She had dressed in jeans and a red sweater; in her purse, she had a change of clothes which she would dispose of before leaving. Maxim was sitting at a table in the rear of the room; he motioned for Abby. Feeling somewhat reluctant as an afterthought, Abby walked toward the table with excitement and worry. Maxim smiled and said, "my love, I am so happy we could find time to be together." Should we go upstairs now, or would you like a drink? No, I don't want to be here. I want to go to the room.

Maxim prepared as usual for their rendezvous'. Abby gladly accepted a glass of wine then excused herself to the restroom. She removed the negligee from her purse and put it on without giving the procedure another thought. When Abby entered the bedroom, Maxim was lounging on the bed in a robe provided by the hotel. Я дар речи моя любовь вы видение вот. (I am speechless, my love you are a vision to behold.) *Oh, Maxim, I love it when you speak Russian!*

The next hour was total sexual bliss for both Abby and Maxim. He was hoping she wouldn't bring up the Luke business, but she did, so he had no choice but to tell her that he did indeed kill the man. Abby told Maxim she suspected as much, and although she did not condone killing anyone, she appreciated that he did what he said he would do. Abby had to tell Maxim she could no longer see him; it was too dangerous for both. She was fearful about how he would take the news, but she had no choice in the matter they're relationship was over.

Abby took the opportunity to convey to Maxim that she would no longer be able to see him that things with Jim and Colin were heating up in his regard. What do you mean by that, Abby? I mean, it's dangerous for us to be together. I don't want to die, and I'm telling you Colin will kill you and probably me as well. No, my love, he will not; I would not allow that to happen. Maxim, I am merely a mid-western woman in a small town. I have found myself surrounded by secret agents, assassins, etc.

this is not the life I want for my daughters and me. I am sorry I have loved being with you, but this is the last time we cannot continue, please try to see this from my viewpoint.

Maxim knew she was right, but he loved her, deep down, he expected her to leave Colin. That was never happening on so many levels. He was a heartbroken man. Could I force her to keep the relationship going by blackmailing her? Yes, but that is not me I don't want to force any woman to be with me better to get this over with now.

Of course, Abby, my love, you are correct in your assessment of our situation. I cannot believe I have found a woman I love but cannot have. With time I will forget you, but always remember if this was another time another place possibly we could have made it work. Abby, my love you have my word, I will not pursue our relationship any longer, but what I cannot promise is that my short tenure with the FBI will end well. You should go now before I change my mind.

With that, Abby dressed but not before kissing Maxim on the cheek with a few tears flowing from her beautiful eyes. She noticed he was choking up a bit as well. As she left, she said, "there are so many things I love about you and so many things I don't, but Maxim I have no regrets."

After Abby left, Maxim stayed behind; he had much on his mind. Did Abby hear him on the phone when he was at her house? He sensed that she might have Abby wasn't a stupid woman; if she told her husband about the conversation with Nikolai, this was her way of letting me know. She didn't have to do this, but she did, and that spoke volumes about how much she cares. Why does love need to end in this manner? Reminding Max that this is why men in his line of work should never get involved.

Surely she knows I would never hurt her or her family. But "The Snowman" was another thing altogether; I make no promises there. I need to contact my superiors and have an exit in place if required. How Jim handles this will tell the tale.

If Abby did indeed tell her husband about the call, Maxim

thought he could talk his way out of It. He would confess right up front that he called a friend he knew in Costa Rica and wanted to see if they could meet up. Weak yes, but so are these Ameri-can's; after all, there is more than one Nikolai in this world.

By the time Abby got home Colin was finished with business. He asked if she wanted to go out for dinner somewhere nice, but she declined. How about we stay home light a fire and eat by the fireplace? That sounds lovely, darling; I'll plan something for dinner while you rest. Thanks pops I am a bit tired.

Balance it all, cover it up, tell a lie, keep the secrets...

Abby researched the time difference between her and Blake; she could call him now, and it would not be too late. Reaching for her phone, Abby decided she would not bring up the fact that Luke was dead. If Blake knew he would say so and then well, she would see where things went from there. Why the hell was she so nervous? Abby thought there was a chance he would not answer, and she hoped that was not the case. After the fourth ring, it went to his voicemail. She left him a message urging him to please call her that it was an emergency; then, as an afterthought, she also asked him to forgive her.

Would he call her back? Could she blame Blake for not returning her call? Surely when he saw the call was marked urgent, he would call if he thought the emergency could be someone he knew.

Colin called Abby for dinner when Abby came into the living room he had pillows on the floor with a beautiful fire burning. Wow pops you've outdone yourself; this looks amazing, and I am famished. Darling, this is so nice and thus far relaxing. The food looks yummy. I'm still surprised you can cook so well. I was a bachelor for many years, so I had no choice in the matter either I cooked or ate out, and that gets boring after a while.

After a few glasses of wine, Abby snuggled up close to Colin and said, "how's you back pops?" My back feels a little tight tonight darling would you want to massage it, so it feels better. Do I look like a physical therapist pops? Oh, come on now, Abby, I sure could use a massage? All right then, but I will need you to remove your shirt so I can get to the sore spots. Better yet, darling, I think lying flat on the bed would make for a much better approach to a massage, don't you agree?

Abby was fast asleep when her phone rang; she jumped out of bed, hoping she didn't wake Colin. Shit, it's Blake, she went downstairs to take the call. Blake, thanks for returning my call I wasn't sure you would. I was reluctant to call Abby, but you did say it was an emergency, so what happened? The main reason for my call was to talk about Rachel, now don't hang up Blake. Rachel and I have talked about this whole mess, so we have an understanding. And she apologized to Colin and me for her involvement.

Blake, I wanted to ask you even though I know you wouldn't, but could you please not tell anyone about Rachel and her involvement? Of course, Abby, I would not do anything to hurt your girls, shit I've known them since they were born. I appreciate that, Blake. How have you been doing, Blake? Well, this is no vacation, I was considering moving closer to my family, but that's no longer what I want. I'm glad to hear that Blake everyone here would miss you, especially me, Blake. That's not the impression I got the last time I saw you, Abby. I know, and I am sorry for that please come home and let me make it up to you. Are you sure Abby because if you feel sorry for me, that's no reason for us to pick up where we left off?

I do not feel sorry for you, Blake, and I am trying my best to keep my life in balance, but I need you to balance it out. I want to believe you, Abby; I can't allow you to hurt me any longer, so when I return, we need to have a civilized conversation about our relationship. That I can do, we will set the boundaries and make a plan that we both can agree. I need to go now. Blake, let me know when you get back? I love you; Abby see you soon.

Who the fuck are you talking to, Abby?

Colin! Yes, your husband, the person you made love to a mere three hours ago. I was talking to Blake; you told me to call him, so I did. Well, that conversation did not sound like I assumed it would. What the hell do you mean by that, Colin? It seemed like two lovers planning to meet. You are crazy, Colin; it was nothing of the kind, and you know it. Blake is my friend, and he is friends with my friends; we miss him being here. There is nothing sinister about that. Other than that, the conversation was mostly about Rachel and that he would never do anything to hurt her. So he had no problem never discussing the matter with anyone ever.

Pops, this discussion is over now, go back to bed before I throw you out of my house. I am becoming bored with your jealousy and accusations. I know what I heard Abby, and that was not the conversation of friends, so when you're ready to confess to what degree your relationship with Blake is, we will talk about it then. I heard you say it, Abby, "I need you here to balance out my life." So what Colin it was an innocent remark made to a friend that with him here, it might balance out my life in this hell hole of drama I'm living.

Again pops for the last time Blake is a lifelong friend, a close friend as all of my group of friends are, being close apparently is something you cannot relate too. I'm going to bed Abby, but I will be in the spare room, I've had enough of this "friends crap for one night." Fine with me Colin, is this how it's going to be married to you, I never took you for the jealous type, insecure and making unfounded threats of infidelity. I'm beyond disappointed!

Of course, my husband is correct, but I'll go to my grave denying any wrongdoing.

Abby was pissed; she went to the liquor cabinet and made herself a stiff drink. Men, I do believe I could become celibate! These men in my life are killing me; they all want me; they all make demands, but when I try to balance all of them, it backfires. Well, things should be easier now that Maxim is out of the picture. I will miss the Russian! Maxim was a shot of adrenalin to my ego. Thank goodness I didn't say anything naughty to Blake, or I would be in deep shit. I can't blame Colin for being upset, but in reality, I said nothing that would indicate I was having an affair with Blake.

Abby fell asleep on the sofa with her glass of wine in her hand. Colin, not being able to sleep, quietly went into the bedroom, and she wasn't there. He walked downstairs to see where Abby was, and when he saw her sleeping. My god, she is so beautiful what would I do without her? Why am I so jealous of that pretty boy I know he isn't her type? I might go so far as to say he might be gay. Which, in my eyes, I would not mind in the least? Abby and her fricking friends are pains in my ass, but she sure loves them all, and apparently Blake's at the top of that list.

Colin picked Abby up and carried her to the bedroom, their bed. Never mind how much it hurt. He kissed her cheek and couldn't stop staring at his beautiful wife. Undressing her, he then got in bed next to her, holding his darling Abby tight until she woke up. You are my one and only pops, why are you so jealous of that guy, he is nothing to me but a friend. I know darling I'm so sorry for my behavior. It won't happen again; you have my word on that.

Abby and Colin made love again, then fell fast asleep.

When Colin found his way to the kitchen, Abby had the coffee brewing, and he smelled the aroma of bacon and eggs. Darling, this is a pleasant surprise I'm famished. Pops, I want to invite my parents over for dinner, or we could go out, it has been way too long. Maybe the girls would come along as well. Good idea Abby; let me know when so I can pencil it in my schedule. Oh, brother, aren't we just the busy man. I am because some pertinent issues need to be addressed and soon. Like? Maxim for one, Rachel's mess, and then there is my own company business of which I have ignored. It sounds like a lot to contend with pops, but I am going to talk to the closing company today, and hopefully, we can close on the house tomorrow. Nothing would make me happier darling, check-in later today so we can plan dinner.

Jim did not want to meet with Maxim in his office; too many ears available just in case the conversation went south. It would not be suitable for his career if it became known that one of his "operatives" went double. Jim doubted this was the case no matter what Colin thought. Could Maxim be considered damaged goods by his superiors? KGB agents don't get caught.

When Maxim entered the restaurant, he could see that Jim did not look so happy. Shit, let's get this over with now. Max, "are you ready for your assignment?" Of course, I am, why wouldn't I be ready, Jim." Just checking, that's all. Let's order, and then we need to talk. They both ordered a steak with the works. Jim, I need to tell you something, and I'm not sure how you will react. What's that mean? React? When I found out where my assignment was, I texted an old Harvard classmate of mine that lives in Costa Rica. I wanted to see if we could meet halfway for a meal if it worked out.

No reaction from Jim yet? Nikolai doesn't live anywhere near where I'm going, Jim, so I didn't feel like it would be a problem. "Are you fucking kidding me," says Jim. You breached this special ops assignment by attempting to make fucking dinner arrangements with a college buddy. Are you out of your mind Maxim, let me ask you this, "what would your Russian superiors say about this plan of yours?" Maxim sat there and said," I would be dead already." Exactly, now for some crazy reason, I believe your story. Why would you make a call like that in Colin's house knowing Abby was there if it wasn't above board? I will send a text telling my friend I will not be able to make it this time. I am sorry for making such an error in judgment, Jim; it won't happen again. Run anything like that through me before making plans while on assignment, Max. You leave early tomorrow, so get some rest now before I change my mind and lock you up.

Abby saved my ass and possibly my life, God I'm going to miss that woman. That situation was too close for comfort. I've got to be more careful going forward. I need to convince Jim that I should operate out of D.C. only.

Chapter 13

Rachel couldn't wait to see Colin and Abby. Do they know what happened to Luke? Who would do such a thing, and why? Suicide? Rachel doubted that's what happened, but what the hell did she know? She only knew him casually. One of her mom's school buddies. I'm not sorry he's dead because now I might have that monkey off my back. Luke was the only link other than my dad, who knows of my involvement. I trust Blake, mom, and Colin; they're not talking.

Blake was packing for his flight home. Thank goodness he decided not to rent out his house. Blake did not want to return to work until he was positive; he could focus only on his job. Even though Abby gave him an element of hope, he still had not made up his mind to continue where they left off. Abby made it clear to him that she was never leaving Colin, so he could not see sense in continuing their painful relationship.

Planning on entering therapy once home Blake knew it would be almost impossible for him to stop seeing Abby cold turkey. If she pursued him, he would evaluate at that time if the proposal was sincere or out of pity. Often he felt she did indeed continue to see him because she felt sorry for him. But he knew he was one of the best lovers' or even the best. Blake knew he was easy on the eye and that she always commented on that trait. He knew he could never compete with her husband's wealth. Just google his name, and his company comes up as a multi-million-dollar enterprise over and over. But Blake doubts being wealthy impresses Abby.

Maxim thought he might text Abby and let her know he and Jim worked things out. Did she care? He thought she did, or she would not have tipped him off in the way she did.

Okay, this man is in some form of delusion Abby did no such thing!

Immediately after Jim met with Maxim, he called Colin and

filled him in. It didn't please Colin that Jim fell for Maxim's weak explanation. Colin knew that Nikolai was a member of the Russian Special Police and an operative currently working out of Costa Rica. Auggie confirmed that he was indeed the man in Erik's photos. No chance it was some college friend; that is such bullshit Colin couldn't believe Jim fell for that crap.

Auggie asked Diego' to meet him in Colin's office for a meeting. He then explained what was going on with a possible infiltration by the Russians. "Keep the surveillance active on Otto, Diego'." Hey, boss, is the boss returning soon? Hell, if I know Diego' and I told you to stop calling me boss. Okay, boss, but graduation is soon; will he be here for that? Diego' I have no idea, but I don't think so, we made arrangements for Colin to use virtual online video conferencing. That's a mouth, full boss! Better than nothing Diego' now, let's go to dinner. Sounds good to me, boss. Jesus stop calling me that!

Abby arranged for her family to meet on Sunday for dinner at Ginny's. Everyone agreed to attend even Rachel and without an argument. Abby was so pleased she was beside herself. Abby got the news that she and Colin should be at the new house that evening for a walkthrough. Wow, that's not much notice, but she was anxious to get moved. Abby texted Colin and told him to meet her at the house by five. He texted back, "are we packed?" She replied, "did you see boxes in our house?" Another text, "no, I did not!" She replied, "well, get busy then pops because we're moving." Back and forth, texting led to this...hire packers and movers immediately!

Colin met Abby at The Mall Bar, had a drink, said goodbye to her friends, and off they went. Abby asked if he was excited about moving? Darling, you have no idea how badly I want to leave your little but lovely home. Good to know pops because when they pulled up to a colossal security gate, Abby pulled out her phone entering a code, and the gate opened wide. Good, grief Abby; when did they put that thing up? Do you like pops? It's a bit over the top, but I like it.

Colin was so impressed with the house and the security system his company installed. It was the most current and state of the art system available. He thought they would be very safe inside and out. The builder rolled his eyes and thought to himself, "who the hell are these people?" Once the walkthrough was over, the builder brought out the dreaded paperwork for signatures. When Colin noticed the final price, he almost dropped his pen. Abby, can I see you alone for a minute, please. Abby sensed that possibly her husband was ticked off about the final price.

Darlin, when I told you to build whatever home you wanted, and money was no object, at any point did I say to you I do not wish to break into a bank to get the money? Well pops not in so many words, but I do encourage you to review the itemized breakdown of costs. Colin proceeds to read line by line until he gets to the line for the value of the security system. Yes, the very system he invented, and his own company installed then charged him over a million dollars. Colin was speechless while Abby smiled in the most smirky way. He then laughed and said, "sign the damn papers Abby."

Even though their new home cost over two and a half million dollars, it was not pretentious or estate-like. They loved it and immediately planned to move as soon as they could get packed.

All new furniture pops we need new furniture for our fresh start in life. Abby, for god's sake, haven't we spent enough money already? No, we have not, and what the hell is wrong with you? Geez, darling, I'm just kidding you're right; of course, we need new everything and bigger. Except for the bedroom, we're keeping that right? Yes, Colin.

Heading back to The Mall Bar and back to Abby's friends, back to high school flashbacks. Colin was still in disbelief that these people (friends), after many years, are still gathering for banter and drinks. He was sure if asked, he couldn't remember a single person he went to high school with, let alone continue to see them fifteen years later. Well, for him, it would be twenty-five years later. Regardless she loved it, and they loved her; she is like a princess or a movie star in their eyes. Prom queen still reigns. The only thing missing was pretty boy Blake. My exercise for the night was to see if anyone brought up his name and if someone does other than Abby, I will forever forget about that frat guy.

Upon leaving, they all congratulated both Abby and Colin on their new home, and then here it comes ta-da—oh Abby David says, "it's unfortunate Blake isn't here to share your good news. I know he would be so happy for you guys." And there it is the final nail in my green coffin buried in the cemetery for jealous lovers. Colin couldn't wait to exit Abby's favorite watering hole.

Pops, I suspect you do not like my friends or my happy hour facility? Not true, Abbs, I do like Amy and David, and the others are okay as well. If you say so, but I do wish you would lighten up about Blake, he will be home soon, and I am sure we will go to the bar to celebrate the upcoming wedding. I am hoping you will not cause issues for my friends and me. All good, Abby, it's all good.

Colin had a doctor's appointment, and possibly he would be cleared to return to work. Knowing he would not be able to return to Costa Rica, he planned to have some serious discussions with Auggie. First-order was preparing for the recruits to receive their credentials and awards. Secondly was to get this house packed and ready for moving day, which could not happen soon enough. Colin was of the mind that since moving into Abby's home, they both had nothing but bad luck. He was not a superstitious person, but things had to change, and moving was a step in the right direction.

It was late evening, and Abby told Colin when he finished with his calls to put on his swim trunks. What the hell Abby I am doing no such thing. Pops, please, I am going out to the patio with my wine, and I am getting into the spa. Colin thought to himself, "spa, my wife and wine." It can't be anything but a good time.

Abby tried to remember the last time she used her sauna, then regretted thinking about that time not so long ago with Blake. Jesus Abby get a grip! When Colin walked out of the house, he found his wife sitting in the sauna butt naked. Pops, what took you so long? Darling, for one thing, I have no idea where my swim trunks are, so it took me a while to find. Colin smiled and asked Abby where her suit was and why she wasn't wearing one? Oh, pops when did the romance end for you?

Colin removed his swimsuit and stepped into the spa. This, my darling, is how our evenings should be. Speaking of sauna's, I don't recall seeing one at our new house? On its way pops, that wasn't something the builder does. You did a great job managing the building that house darling; it is fantastic, and I love how it turned out — speaking of homes Colin in reality, how much time will be spending in Gary? I would expect we will be here more than half the time and in Chicago sometimes. It's dumb to go back and forth, but for now, being here is fine with me until I figure out the rest of my life.

Amy phoned Abby to discuss a few details of the wedding, which was a mere two weeks away. Abby assured her she and Colin had their clothes fitted and were to pick them up the day before the wedding. Abby then proceeded to tell Amy about the upcoming bachelorette party details. Abby wanted the party to be special for her friends, especially since she has pretty much evaded their company for such a long time.

Blake arrived back in the states, and while riding in the uber, he knew he was looking forward to going home. His trip was shorter than he wanted, but he felt it served its purpose. Avoiding any contact with Abby and or his friends was a test of his will, which he wasn't sure he had any left. Blake knew he needed to see his therapist and regularly. She wouldn't be happy with him if he insisted that his relationship with Abby was going to continue. The therapy was to help him overcome his obsession, not extend it.

On the day after the sauna bath, Colin and Abby were slightly hungover. Too much to do without worrying about feeling like shit. Abby knew Blake would be home today, and she was concerned about Colin's doctor's appointment, not going as well as he thought it should. Then, of course, there was the incident involving her daughter. Who shot Luke? What was Colin's plans for the future? Too much to think about for such a beautiful morning.

Colin was swaggering down the stairs rubbing his head, trying to relieve his headache. Coffee was much needed, but oh what a night it was, and his back was feeling just fine. Possibly he was on the verge of a complete recovery. Now what? Back to work fulltime or not? Chicago or work out of the office near home? Shit too much to think about this morning.

Abby found Colin in the kitchen with his coffee and making toast. Hey pops, how are you feeling on this lovely morning? Same as you darlin hungover and happy. Ain't that the truth pops. It was a fantastic night. With a smiley face, Colin replies, "yes, it was." Come here, woman I need a hug and nothing else. Very funny pops, we need to start packing today, so call a moving company and have them here Saturday. Darling, you are so bossy, but I love it.

Chapter 14

Maxim landed in Costa Rica with this cloud of doubt hanging over his head. He never felt so out of sorts about his place as a professional. Not necessarily his ability to perform but his position within. Being captured here still haunted him, and now he was on the other side about to bring another fellow agent to the surface not to capture but to assassinate. Being a double agent sucked not only was he always watching his back, but everyone around him potentially might figure out that he was. That phone call at Abby's was a close call, and he vowed never to assume his surrounding was safe. His thoughts were not where they should be, focusing on his assignment; the problem was Abby; he just could not get her out of his head.

Auggie was on "all systems go" regarding Otto, the spy. Colin provided the heads up on the FBI spy-ring operation. He also knew that Maxim was the lead on the assignment, which was beyond a surprise. Auggie concluded that in the end, Maxim being here in Costa Rica made sense. He knew who the players were and possibly knew more than Jim. Even though Maxim was incognito, Auggie was thankful for the intel. This recruiting class could not end fast enough. Then what, his career depended on tasks and assignments from Centry Security, the question was, "is Colin running the company?"

Wearing a Chicago Cubs baseball cap and dressed as "American," as was possible, Maxim blended in as a tourist. He planned to do a tropical forest excursion near the camp. Allowing him to get closer to the camp in hopes of finding his mark. Many things could blow his cover, so remaining unseen was key to finding the Russian spy. So blending in with the tourist group was critical. Then there is this, "where the hell was Nikolai?" If my intuition is on spot, he is here, where is the question? Nikolai would surface when he so desired.

Maxim needed to connect with Auggie if, for no other reason, he needed the schedule so he could find this asshole quickly. Jungles are not my thing, the bigger the city, the better, that is my element. With the tour starting soon, Maxim contacted Auggie and received the information to track down his mark. All he needed to do was walk away from the tour group for a few minutes when close enough to the camp.

Bugs, mud, foliage hitting me in the face was enough to put me over the edge "get me the hell out of this hell?" Then within my sights was the mark running alone along the path just as Auggie said he would. I attached the silencer aimed ready to shoot when all of a sudden, the weapon was knocked out of hand by, "what the fuck Nikolai are you doing here?" My friend, the question is, "what the fuck are you doing trying to kill my agent?"

Totally stunned, Maxim says, "what the hell do you mean, your agent?" Max, we need to talk but not here. Meet me at that café in town. What café? That would be the only one Max be there around midnight. With that awkward situation ended, Max is beside himself with so many unanswered questions.

Blake sent Abby a secure message using his burner phone she gave a while back. As ridiculous and funny as he thought her cautions were, he believed that Abby would resort to any methods of communication to hide her affair. Whatever she wanted him to do, he would. The text was simple, "Abbs, I would love to see you; let's meet?" Simple, short, and to the point. Just like she wants.

Blake's therapist suggested, or should I say, insisted that he end his ongoing affair with Abby. The sooner, the better was her exact words. Emphasizing how critical it might be to his health and safety. *An exaggeration hell no!* Blake was of the impression their relationship was almost to the ending point, but he wanted to find out if it was possible to reignite that fire. He would patiently wait for a response.

Was his therapist right in her analysis of Colin and what he is capable of doing? According to Abby, Colin and his talents should never be taken for granted. Abby did indeed know enough about his abilities, along with the fear she sees in others when they are around him. Abby insists these fears are not rumor nor hearsay. In his mind, Blake believed with all his heart that she was worth any possibility of being caught. They have always exercised on the side of caution, before Colin and since.

But Blake felt something in the pit of his stomach. The intuition of sorts that told him Colin could see right through their lies.

Moving along with his uneventful life was his goal with or without Abby. Getting back to work and reconnecting with his friends also a priority. Blake called David to get the latest update on the wedding plans; Blake gave David and Amy his word that he would return home before the wedding events started. *Shit, I wonder if Abby has told Colin that he was in the wedding party? Probably not!*

Unless Blake heard otherwise, he assumed he would not see Abby before the rehearsal dinner. He was hopeful Abby would respond to his message saying she would meet. He thought seeing her legitimately with her husband in their presence, was somehow a bit exciting.

And dangerous idiot!

Blake was clearing his house of the dust and grit that seemed to find every nook and cranny during his absence. He ordered groceries online, he had his laundry cleaned and delivered, and now he would go to the gym to workout. Keeping in shape was a priority; the one thing he knew was that Abby was in perfect shape, and she had no use for any man in her life who wasn't. *No flab for Abb! Oh, brother!*

As he left the house, his phone binged, a text message from Abby, thank god. "Blake would love to meet but cannot confirm a day or time we are moving tomorrow, will get back to you asap." Shit! Blake replied, "let's meet before the rehearsal; can't wait to see you." Abby replied, "sounds good I have to leave before Colin, so this will work out, meet me at the hotel, you know where be there at 4 pm exactly, get a room, text me the number."

I must admit I have missed Blake greatly!

Seriously Blake never expected that to happen holy shit; I am doing the happy dance. I need to go shopping again. I want to wear something new and youthful; she needs a young man, not that old guy.

Colin saw Abby typing away on her phone and asked who she was texting so early. Wedding texts pops no end to them. Speaking of the event, I have finalized your flight plans for the party, and there will be a limo waiting at LaGuardia to take you, girls, to the restaurant. The driver will remain outside of every venue so he can keep an eye out. Oh, pops, you have thought of everything, and I thank you. Well, you ladies have a good time and don't be too hard on Tom. He is a pilot, not a plaything Abby. Really, well, he is too good-looking pops, so I make no promises.

The never-ending Costa Rician takedown!

Maxim was thinking out loud, "What the fuck is going on with this assignment?" How am I supposed to operate when my intelligence officers don't forward the specifics of an operation? This situation is a cluster-fuck! And it appears that Nikolai wasn't informed either. I fear this could be departmental infighting. One agency wanting to outdo the other, but in this case, we all lose. Nikolai and I will get to the bottom of this tonight. I find that this "double agent" shit sucks, and I can see why others want no part of it. Almost busted by Abby, which puts me in jeopardy with the Americans, and now I am forced to address my superiors' methods. Going rogue is starting to sound good.

Seeing the glass half full, I could have killed that kid, our own recruit, and I could have been executed for that mishap.

I found Nikolai sitting at a table towards the back door. My first thoughts were, "this is the worst looking excuse of a café I have ever seen." There was a bottle of vodka sitting on the table and two glasses. I feared for my life drinking or eating in this poor excuse of a dining establishment, but Nik seemed to be at home. Maxim, I ordered dinner, have some vodka in the meantime. I sat down, wiping the chair seat off first, Nikolai laughed enjoying my dread.

Наконец он был он сидеть ваши русские задницу вниз Макс! (Finally, he had had it sit your Russian ass down Max!) С радостью, "теперь скажите мне, почему вы здесь?" (Gladly, "now tell me why you are here?") Кто ты такой, чтобы спрашивать меня о том, что ты уже должен знать? (Who are you to ask me something you should already know?) Who am I? *I am the Russian double agent fucking spy that wasn't informed* about you being here and that I was not supposed to kill the guy. Am I clear, Nikolai? And please speak English only. Fine, okay, I will find out from my department head where this assignment went wrong. I could have killed that kid Nik then how would our leaders feel about that? I would end up being hunted as a criminal and could never go home. You make me laugh, Maxim, not your fault this happened, of that I am sure.

Otto will be recruited by me before the end of the day tomorrow. My assignment was to deliver him home shortly thereafter. Now I hope that the operation has not been thwarted by the American's.

No worries there, Nikolai. I will merely tell them my mission was successful. They'll need proof, of course. Let me take care of that, Max. I will have him play out a death fall from the mountain range above the jungle. Pictures of the same. Let's meet tomorrow Max, right here for an early breakfast to finalize our plan.

Chapter 15

Moving day, thank god. Abby and Colin were wide awake by sunup. The coffee pot is the only item not packed at Colin's insistence. The movers were to arrive any time now. Colin asked, "darling, you gonna miss this place?" No, not really, the girls said they would live here. I'm okay with that, but no, I can't wait to get the hell out. Colin wondered to himself if that were true. He hoped it was because he was making lifestyle changes right and left to please his wife. After this move, and then the wedding and graduation is over, he wanted to return to work. The sooner, the better.

Abby had to understand his company was his baby, his belief that he was doing some good in this crazy world. Dangerous, of course, necessary absolutely. Colin had his mind made up; he was returning to his position fulltime, he would agree to curtail the traveling as much as possible. He would tell Abby in a few days when things calmed down.

The move did not take long; most of the furniture was staying for the girls to use. Abby did not want any of it except the bedroom furniture. Amanda met her mom at the house later that day to retrieve the keys and other items she might need. Mom, you seem sad. No sweetie, not sad this is just another step-in life; this house is not for Colin and me. We needed our own place a fresh start. You girls can stay here as long as you want, of course, I will expect some rent payments once you get a job. Mom, I wouldn't have it any other way. Now I'm leaving Amanda. I'm starving, and I'm sure Colin is as well.

When Abby returned to the new house, Colin had his boxes unpacked; of course, it was mostly items for his office. He was expecting his clothes and other things to be delivered anytime now from Chicago. Abby thought he was foolish to sell his condo in Chicago. Colin said, "if we are starting over, let's do it all the way." How much time would they spend in the windy city Abby had no idea, but for now, she didn't care to speculate.

Darling, I am starving; how about a nice dinner to celebrate our move? Sounds great pops, where do you want to go? Your choice Abby. What about happy hour at The Mall Bar? Oh god, I would rather not, I want real food, not bar food. Okay, let's go to Ginny's on Main then. Excellent choice, are you ready to go darling? Yes! Abbs, where are the instructions for the security system? Pops, I installed the app on your phone. Use the app to manage the system, or you can do it manually from the keypad. Jesus Abby, can you set it for now then show me how to use it later on. Pops, you need to get your head into the 21st century!

They had a quiet dinner with a bottle of wine to boot. Colin was tired, so it didn't take much alcohol to loosen him up. Loose lips as the saying goes.... Abby, I want to talk about what happens next. What does that mean pops? Darling, I need *no what I mean is* I want to get back to work, like an in-person work environment — not working via my phone and email. Colin, what are you talking about specifically? I don't want to work from home nor the local office, which is for Joe to manage. And? I need to get back to my office in Chicago, darling.

Abby was fuming, and it showed. Now darling, don't be upset; surely, you didn't think I could continue being here fulltime. I own a company; I have employees Abby; it's my business, and I need to manage it, which involves being at the helm. I get it Colin I really do, but we have an agreement if you remember, running the company is a given but the constant traveling that is not going to happen. You promised pops! I did, and I will do my best to keep that promise, I will not assign myself to any lengthy assignments, but there may be shorter trips a day or two here and there. Alright Colin, if this is what you want, then I'm good with it. But know this I also am going back to work, I can't merely sit around all day, I'm too young to retire, unlike you. Very funny, darling ha-ha. Now, how about we head home and continue this banter in bed. It's been a long day for old folks pops I suppose you're very sleepy. *Ready for bed, yes, tired no, horny, yes!*

Blake had been shopping all day; he wanted to make an impression, a lasting one. He did not want to appear as mundane as he probably was. So he made an appointment with a "personal assistant." Wow and wow was all he could muster up after he saw his new image in the mirror. Damn, he was downright handsome; along with some current trendy clothes, he thought there was no way Abby could resist his charm. Next Friday could not get here fast enough. Blake had already made the room reservation, the best suite they had was the honeymoon suite, and he hoped Abby would not object to being pampered.

Blake did confess to his therapist that he was meeting Abby (*the therapist does not know Abby's name*) and insisted he keeps his expectations at a minimum. What if the woman isn't there for sex? What if she's breaking it off? No, Blake assured her that was not the case; the room is for romance and sex nothing else. His therapist just shook her head in total disapproval, then said, "I hope for your mental wellbeing she meets your expectations?" She has, in every way, doctor. Blake, you have set the bar so low for this relationship. And the reason for that is you know it can't end the way you want.

Nikolai and Maxim met for breakfast so they could finalize a plan of action. Nik asked Otto to meet them so they could inform him of the "look like your dead plan." These two senior operatives somewhat amused Otto, but none the less he knew what he needed to do. Maxim set up the place and time for the plot to begin, he and Nikolai agreed to meet later that day for another disgusting dinner. Nikolai was in charge of the extraction process, which would occur immediately after the faked death.

No one in the American intelligence community knew that Maxim was an actual double agent. Against Jim's decision from the beginning, Colin believes Maxim is still a spy for the mother country. So Jim sending Maxim to assassinate Otto could be the end of Jim's career unless the assignment is a success.

Erik's intuition that Otto was indeed another Russian who had eluded not only the camp leaders but Colin. Auggie advised Erik of the plan to eliminate him instead of trying to turn him. Erik agreed but wanted to know why. Auggie explained that Colin did not want someone so young and inexperienced. Stressing that they had recently turned a high-ranking Russian, it was not useful for their programs to do so again. Auggie further explained that Colin was against the turning of the other spy. Empathizing Colin's priority was to prevent this invasion from ever happening again.

Colin swore this was the last fucked up recruit class and even thought about moving the location to another country. With Amanda more than likely in the next group of recruits, Colin wanted the process to run smoothly.

The bride to be, Abby and eight of their friends, departed for New York. Tom was tipped off by Colin to keep all the ladies safe, along with professionally behaving himself. Tom replied, "boss, we are talking about your wife and her friend's correct?" Yes, is that a problem, Tom? Oh no, of course not, but I don't want to be responsible if things get out of hand. No worries, Tom; my wife is a pussycat! Tom rolled his eyes as he walked to the airplane for what he thought would be the ride of his life.

Tom picked up his microphone and announced. "ladies we are ready for takeoff, please fasten your seat belts." And he wanted to add as he made the cross, "please be good so that I can keep my job." Then, "ladies, I turned off the fasten your seatbelt sign." You may now move around the cabin. All of a sudden, Tom hears laughing loud girly laughing. Too much laughing, he requested his assistant to the cockpit for a report. Stella, please tell me the ladies are behaving in a manner of which will not get me fired? Relax Tom; all is good back there; the girls are just having fun. So says you, Stella, I've heard rumors about that woman; evidently, she's hell on wheels. Good grief Tom, you are such a prude. No, Stella, I am not; remember I have seen Abby in action; on one trip, she actually seduced him, and they had sex in the back. NO! Yes, I could hear them all the way up here. Jesus Tom just fly the plane.

Colin thought being alone for a couple of days would be peaceful and quiet. It was all of that and more, the more being bored, lonely, and missing his wife. So much has happened in the last year that Colin found it hard to revisit all of the events without laughing out loud even though none of it was funny. Who would have thought meeting that beautiful woman in a bar would lead me sitting in a new villa like home, married, two stepdaughters, and an office in the smallest city I have ever lived? I need some company someone to join me for dinner. Some male company, of course. Colin called Joe, who asked if Marty could join them. Of course Joe, but please do not tell me you want to go to the Mall Bar! Joe laughed and said, "not my cup of tea Colin."

The three men started with a nice dinner, and then Colin asked Joe if he wanted to see their new home. I would love to see the finished product, Colin. Afterall I helped Abby from the beginning with the planning in your absence. Great, then how about a few hands of cards. Marty said, "a man after my heart, I love to play cards." Joe jumped in and said, "ha, that man is not your type Marty." Smiles all around, except Colin, he just rolled those baby blues.

Joe followed Colin to the house; they pulled into a private drive about a mile long, ending with a ginormous security gate. They waited for Colin to input the code so they could enter. Marty said, 'impressive indeed." Joe just rolled his eyes and said, 'over-kill."

Well, Joe, "what do you think?" It's big, and it's massive, but not overstated or pretentious. I like it, and you guys will be happy here. Yes, I believe we will Abby did a great job designing this house. Colin, do you plan on staying in town fulltime, or will you split your time up between here and home office? Nothing is final yet, but yes Joe, I will, or hopefully, we will spend time between both cities as needed. Who will manage our local office, Colin? Well, Joe, that would be you, you will be the operations manager and will a raise in salary as well.

The Captain, aka Tom, let the ladies know that they would be landing and fasten their seatbelts. Upon landing, Tom reminded Abby that the limo was waiting for them and that he would see them at the hotel. Abby seemed to be disappointed hearing that news. Tom, "why are you staying in the same hotel as us, girls"? Orders from the boss. So Colin told you to keep an eye on us? Well, he didn't exactly say it like that, Abby. It was more like, "if anything happens to my wife, you will regret it on more than one level." Oh, for god's sake, Tom, he's a pussycat; don't worry about us. What a coincident Abby he said the same thing about you.

Chapter 16

Maxim woke early; he thought this day could not end soon enough, and it just started. Thinking back to last year and his decision to cave in to the FBI's offer to either become a double agent or die. Now he found himself backstepping about their offer. This covert operation will not end well, no matter the outcome.

Otto and Nikolai stationed at the site, a small waterfall that Otto believed he could safely fall over and still come out alive. Nik placed a little red dye pack on Otto's chest just to be sure the shooting looked legit. When Maxim arrived, Nikolai sensed that he looked apprehensive about this plan. Maxim, "this will work no worries, comrade." Famous last words, my friend. Let's get this over with, so to review, Otto I'm on a foot chase we arrive at the falls, you hesitate just long enough to provide me the opportunity of taking the kills shot then you go over the waterfall. I will then snap a quick photo of you with blood on your body as you go over.

Operation complete. Maxim was now on the way to Washington. Jim opened his secure line, and there it was the photo of Otto now deceased. He forwarded the text to Colin, with a footnote. "operation successful." Colin was pleased, and now his job was to make sure his recruitment program/any programs never had another infiltration of undesirables.

Nikolai stayed behind, waiting for Otto. With only two hours to make it to the extraction point, he was anxious to get going. The jungle was a hindrance; Nikolai hated every second of this assignment. He and Maxim had many things to talk about, and he wanted to get that meeting out of the way as soon as possible. As soon as Otto was safely transported to Moscow, Nikolai would arrange the meet with Maxim. He would make clear to his comrade that he needed to decide his fate, keep spying on American soil as a double-agent or try to return to Foreign

Intelligence as a decorated officer. Nik was sure the latter option would end up as a "dead-end" for his friend.

With the arrangements made, all Blake could do was wait. The rehearsal dinner was this Friday a mere three days that will seem like a hundred. He wasn't sure what to expect from their liaison, but he knew what he wanted it to be; a few hours of romantic ecstasy. Deep down, Blake knew Abby would not have had him get a room just to have a conversation. He knew her that well, so he paid no heed to the warnings the therapist gave. One thing Blake knew was that if he and Abby continued as they had in the past, it could lead to one or both of them in jeopardy. As always, Blake thought her worthy of being caught. At least that asshole Jim was off their back. *Or so he thought!*

Abby and the girls returned home from New York unharmed and anxious to get on with the wedding events. Colin could not wait for this to be done and over. The house was active with women and wedding attire. Tonight was the rehearsal dinner Abby had to leave early to help set up which gave Colin a few hours of R&R. Abby set out his tuxedo and other items before leaving. For that, he was thankful God knows he wouldn't want to arrive unkemptly.

Abby took everything she needed with her to the hotel so she could finish getting ready. As she drove to meet Blake, her thoughts were not of remorse or guilt but of how excited she was to be with Blake. Absence might make the heart grow fonder, but it also gave her a feeling of euphoric sexual arousal. She could not believe how much she missed him. Knowing she was "again" being unfaithful to her husband, Abby convinced herself that her love for Colin was very different than that for Blake. Being married made the desire for Blake all the more exciting.

Blake was waiting in the lounge; this was the longest day of his life. He hasn't seen Abby in weeks, and the waiting was almost over. When she walked in, Blake stood up and stifled himself from running into her arms but thought that was an immature way to greet a grown woman. Abby sat down, then said, "I'm here; you're here, what are we waiting for." With that, he gently reached for her hand, she happily took his, and they left for the room.

Abby and Blake, for the first time, had forgone any and all evidence of frivolous use of non-essentials, which means no sexy lingerie or other playthings. They both merely removed their clothing, and she helped him as he her. Once on the bed, Blake held Abby for what seemed like a lifetime. Then he smoothed her hair from her face and kissed her with a kiss like none other. Abby, "I have missed you more than I can say, I honestly thought we might not ever be together again." Abby responded with such passion it took Blake by surprise and delight.

Something was different; this was not sex; they were making love, incredible love. They both knew each other well, as they should, twenty years is a long time. With tears in their eyes and almost in unison, Blake and Abby said, "I love you."

Abby suggested that she leave first and told Blake to arrive for dinner an hour later. Upon leaving, Abby kissed Blake and told him she would text him a date and time so they could have a conversation regarding how or if they could manage to be together. Blake asked her, "would you define together, Abby?" If only I could, then we would have all the answers we need.

When Colin arrived, he didn't see Abby, he asked around, but no one knew where she was. Damn, where the hell is that woman? He walked through the lobby, and there she was coming out of the restroom, looking beautiful and radiant. She smiled as she moved closer to her husband, motioning for him to bend down so she could reach him. Then she kissed him with so much passion that Colin almost pulled her into the corner for more. Darling, that was unexpected, and can we leave now? Ha pops, of course not, but the night will not last long. Well, I can't wait to get home and get more of that goodness, darling.

Abby smiled and thought, "there is something seriously wrong with me."

Colin thought Amy and David looked so happy' sitting at the head of the table, surrounded by their friends and family. Inside he wondered if they like Abby would continue to frequent The Mall Bar. What a crazy thought to have at this time, but living here in this close-knit city with residents that have known each other since grade school is something I have never experienced. I doubt I will ever understand it, which is one reason I continue to harbor ill will regarding Abby and Blake's friendship. Just look at that guy, I find him looking Abby's way every chance he gets. Can he be so naïve that he doesn't realize I and everyone else can see him? *Idiot, she's way out of his league!*

On their way home, Abby and Colin reflected on the night's events. Pops, did you have a good time? The food was fabulous, darling, and the bride and groom look very happy. They do don't they pops; you know they have been together since high school. Why have they waited so long to marry Abby? I honestly don't know, maybe he never asked her. You have strange friends Abby. At least I have friends Colin! Yes, you do, and the friends' list is lead by none other than the prom king himself. You sound like a broken record pops, same shit over and over. Sorry, I'm tired and a bit drunk. No excuse you have made it very clear you don't like Blake. No, my darling, I do not.

Once home, Abby was in no mood for romance, but Colin, on the other hand, couldn't wait to get to bed. Abby gave off vibes of no interest, but Colin kept trying until she finally said something she would surely regret. "Colin, please go to sleep; I am not interested in sex tonight." Stunned, Colin replied with a loud voice, "since when Abby?" Colin, a huge turn off is the fact that you continue insinuating that Blake and I have a thing, I recall telling you that if you stayed with that train of thought, it would not end well for you, remember? I vaguely remember your threats, Abby. Well, there you go then; tonight is not ending well for you pops. This conversation is now over go to sleep.

Colin tossed and turned all night, he thought about sleeping in the spare room but was afraid that would send the wrong signal. What's with that guy anyway, I'm just as nice looking, and in great shape, god knows I have more money. My entire career, my intuition, and instincts never failed. I know deep down something is going on with him and my wife. I need to end this shit once and for all. Colin made a mental note to call Jim in the morning; maybe he can shed some light on my nightmare. I know I promised Abby I would let this go, but I can't. I'm not sharing my wife with anyone, let alone that guy.

Saturday was a busy day; Colin knew Abby would be gone most of the day. When he woke up, she was gone already, leaving him a note with instructions along with his evening attire on the bed. After reading the note, he saw the postscript, "pops, if you love me, you will let the Blake issues alone, if you don't, I cannot promise a happy ending." I love you so much, Abby. Shit now what?

The big event was about to start; Colin sat in a pew with Amanda, Rachel, Joe, and his date. All the bridesmaids and groomsmen have entered, including the pretty boy, Blake. Abby was the matron of honor, when she walked in I just melted inside. Amanda took my hand and whispered, "she is worth any amount of agony she causes." Shocked, Colin squeezed her hand and said, "I pray that is a true statement." I've watched her all my life Colin, men love her and she them, but remember one thing she married you and I never thought she would ever remarry. That says,' you are the one and only. Thanks, Amanda, that means a lot. I guess I worry too much about our age difference. Well, stop worrying; she's all in pops. Amanda tried as best she could to reassure Colin, but she doubts he believed a word, poor guy. I do hope mom doesn't fuck over him like the others.

Congratulations all around, and then it was off to the reception, David Invited Colin to join Abby in the limo ride. Of course, he would go, even though Abby had not said a word to him about going. David told him he wasn't the only spouse joining in the fun.

All members of the wedding party and their dates or wives were already in the limo; Colin could not decide to join or not; he felt out of place. Amanda came up next to him and said, "go with her Colin, please if you don't, it's like pushing her away." He nodded in agreement and opened the door to the limo and got in. Abby looked surprised, but she did motion for him to sit next to her. Well, that was a good sign, he thought.

Colin thought he was too old for this crowd, but he went along because he was married to a woman many years younger, accept it, or change it old boy.

As the night progressed, Abby seemed to lighten up and started acting like the woman he knew her to be. They danced, enjoyed excellent food, enjoying the night. A couple of hours into the night the band played a slow song, feeling unusually festive, Colin held his hand for Abby, she accepted, and they walked to the dance floor. He held her close, and she whispered into his ear, "tonight will not end like last night pops, let's put the Blake issues behind us, can you do that." Before Colin could answer none other than Blake walks up to Abby and asks if he could break in for a dance. *David and Amy noticed Blake's bold move and watched with worry.* The look on Abby's face was priceless, oh shit, Amy whispered to David, "I believe our party is about to get interesting." Colin politely refused to hand her over. Blake reached for Abby's hand, but she removed his and asked him to please go away. Again Blake tapped on Colin's shoulder to change partners. Colin ignored him. Blake grabbed Abby's arm aggressively this time.

And the shit hits the fan!

Then Colin said, "son, doing that was the biggest mistake of your life." Abby pulled her hand away, and quickly, Blake reached for it yet again. This time Colin merely removed her hand from his, and then before they knew what was coming, Colin right-handed a punch into Blake's face, and he was on the floor. Not much blood, but he was out cold. It was like a scene from a movie, with awes and many dropped mouths.

Everyone was staring at Blake on the floor. Abby could not believe Colin hit him that hard. *What should I do?* If she ran to Blake, it was trouble for her marriage; if she didn't, Blake would not be happy. Doing nothing sounds just about right.

David got to Blake first, then David's brother, the doctor, took over. Well, the doctor said, "he'll wake in a minute or so." Let's move him to the men's room; there's a sofa in there. Rachel told Amanda, "well, I think that was a long time coming." Indeed it was sister, and this time Blake asked for it. Rachel thought the whole thing was so romantic, in her lifetime, she felt no two men would fight over her. Colin remained seated at their table, which just happened to be the wedding party table. David didn't look happy; Amy shook her head in disbelief. But to all who witnessed the ruckus, they knew Blake asked for the ass beating; why he didn't stop was a mystery.

Abby was crying and trying her best to stay composed as she hurt inside to out. She had to support Colin in this tragedy because, honestly, Blake was wrong. The music started again, and that quieted things down, and within minutes, all were having a good time. Colin prayed Abby would come and sit with him, but he wasn't sure, did he walk over that line, he had no choice but to put Blake in his place. Abby did thankfully return to her seat next to her husband, who breathed a sigh of relief. He reached for her hand, which she gladly allowed. Did fate enter into Abby's life on this night?

Is it possible that Blake entered into a realm so new to him that his life would forever be changed? Did Colin enter into the most critical stage of his life fighting for the woman he loved? Answers to those questions lay with Abby; only she has the power to alter what path she takes with these two men. Must she choose, or can she continue to play with their hearts until one of them falls? *Tonight was a game-changer for Blake, of that she was sure.*

Once home, Colin went directly to the bar for another drink. He asked Abby if she wanted to join him. I think you've had enough to drink Colin and no thank you; I don't want a drink. I am going to take a shower and get to bed. Well that does it she's pissed; I did hit him kind of hard honestly I wish he wouldn't have gotten up at all. Actually, I just might finish that guy off anyway; he's an idiot. But I do give him kudos for being relentless, even if he is the dumbest guy I know.

Colin did not pursue conversation nor offered his body to his wife that night. Sleeping on it seemed to be the right path to take.

Chapter 17

The morning after the wedding and the "punch" debacle Colin found Abby making breakfast, she handed him his coffee cup. He was pleasantly pleased but didn't dare smile. She placed his food in front of him, sat down with her plate, and they ate. Then she started talking, "pops, this Blake business is over, he was wrong, and I can't imagine what came over him." I realized last night that his caring for me has become compulsive and disruptive to my life and, more importantly, our marriage. Now I am asking you to please back off of this subject for good. Can you do that, Colin? *No answer!* Well, I am waiting for an answer Colin, because if you can't let this go, I have no choice but to decide for you. Jesus Colin answer me, please.

I'm eating darling I will answer your question when I finish. Good grief pops!

Now I'm ready to talk. First, I am not sorry I hit the pretty boy. He asked for it, and you know that is a true statement. Secondly, I am happy to put this situation and that man behind us on one condition. I'm listening pops. I want you to tell me if you have had a sexual relationship with Blake? What the hell, Colin, I'm not telling you any such thing! You will, Abby, and if you don't, I am returning to Chicago as soon as I can pack. I am too old for this shit darling, and I will not stand for it one more minute. I love you more than anything, but I will not share my wife with anyone period end of subject Abby.

My, my, pops you are very bossy this morning. No, Abby, I'm not bossy merely a man who needs answers to which I am entitled. So you want to know if Blake and I have had sex, and when I answer that question, no matter you will accept my answer. I said I would even if I don't like what you have to say. Fine, as you well know, Blake and I were a couple in high school; we dated all four years. Blake and I had sex in tenth grade and then every year until I left for college. But I've always dated others, and he was not exclusive. *Imagine that!* He wanted to get married, but I said no. I met Ed in college, and the rest is history until I got divorced.

Okay, that's a lovely story Abby, but you know I am not interested in ancient history. I want to know about the here and now and how long ago did you and he start seeing each other after your divorce. You really are pissing me off Colin, none of that is any of your business. Did I ask you about your love affairs before we met pops, no I did not, nor do I care? Abby answer my question please, it's the right thing to do. I don't like being quizzed Colin, and I resent it immensely. Don't care Abby this elephant has to leave our marriage. Start talking or don't, but I want answer's if I don't get them from you I will from him.

What the fuck Colin, you have lost your mind.

I 'm done pussyfooting around this issue, Abby; we need to put it to rest, and if you don't think I am worthy of some honesty, then I should not be here, be married to you. There has never been another person in my life that I have loved as much as you. I have practically changed my entire lifestyle to be with you, and lately, I feel like I`m your second fiddle. Now start talking, or I am leaving.

Yes, after my divorce, I did start seeing Blake again, casually at first, we always got along. At the start it was only platonic no sex, I wasn't ready for that kind of relationship. After a while, we did start sleeping together, why not we were two adults in a relationship. Then *he wanted more, the whole thing marriage and kids. Obviously, I turned him down, and I might add many times.*

Yet he keeps coming back for more Abby; he is relentless. Yes, he is, but Colin, he and I did date before I met you, but we stopped long before that at least a year before. And since we met Abby? I swear Colin, Blake, and I have not had an intimate relationship for over two years or longer. It is not my fault pops that he can't see my feelings for him are not what his are for me. I have tried and tried to make him understand. Now have I answered your question or not? You have, and I appreciate your honesty Abby, I hope you know this conversation had to happen, I love you, and I want us to be as happy as possible.

Well, that's very kind of you, Colin, but you see I had already answered these very questions on more than one occasion in the past. You choose to disbelieve me then so what assurance do I have that you are finally satisfied this time? I can see your point Abby, and you are right, but only that you have told me in the past. I believe you and for more than one reason, first, when he approached you to break into our dance, you refused; secondly, you were supportive of me after I hit him. I was Colin, Blake was wrong and should not have continued. Last night opened my eyes to his obsessive, compulsive behavior. I didn't see it before, but now I do. I will decide how to handle my friendship with him, but I have no intention of avoiding him altogether, Colin.

I didn't think you would Abby, and I wouldn't ask you to do that, but if he doesn't grasp or understand, I will convince him otherwise. I will handle him, Colin, not you. Make sure you do, and now let's put this behind us, darling.

Abby agreed to move forward as Colin wanted, but at this juncture, she felt defeated by both. A feeling she did not like nor wanted, caught between two lovers, was a place she never thought she would be; well on the wrong side of it anyway. Blake could destroy her marriage by confessing to Colin. After last night she thought he might do just that. She was scared of the outcome none the less, that was why she knew what her next step was.

Maxim received a secure test from none other than Abby. She wanted to know how to reach him. Interesting, he thought, I should ignore her. I don't want to think about her any longer, or I shall never forget how much I love that woman. He waited most of the day before deciding to text her back. *Abby, I will text when I return to the states, look for my message in a few days, sending my affections, Max*

Thank god she thought, he owes me, and he knows it!

Blake spent the night in the ER taken there by David's brother in town for the wedding. Feeling remorse for his actions, Blake wondered if Abby would ever forgive him for his discussing behavior. No, he thought not. The doctor said his jaw was not broken but severely bruised. He asked who hit him because whomever it was knew precisely where and how to apply the blow. Blake told the doctor, "he is someone whom I would never want to be on his bad side." The doctor laughed and replied. "and this is not being on his bad side, young man?" Ha, I think not, but he did not like me asking his wife for a dance. You can go home now but follow up with your primary care doctor in a few days.

Blake called for an Uber ride; he could barely talk and considered himself lucky that that was all the damage he endured. What the hell was I thinking, he thought possibly this might be the end of their relationship. Something had to change that was a given. Her husband is no longer someone he wants to mess with. Regardless Blake knew he owed both of them an apology, and the sooner, the better.

Abby was cleaning up the bedroom when she heard the doorbell ring. Colin was still in the kitchen, so she yelled for him to answer the door. Using the video doorbell for the front door, Colin could not believe his eyes. Jesus does this guy ever give up. He pushed the intercom button for the bedroom and asked Abby to please come down.

Colin opened the door to a pathetic looking, sad man. May I come in, please? Colin motioned for him to do so. "I would like to speak to both of you if I may." Abby saw Blake and almost fainted how horrible and vulnerable he looked. Abby, "Blake wants to talk to us, are you okay with that?" Sure let's go into the living room.

What's up Blake, and why are you here, says Colin? I wanted to apologize for my behavior last night. I do not know what came over me, maybe too much to drink or wishful thinking about that dance. No matter though, it was uncalled for an unforgivable act. Yep that is was Blake, I think I speak for Abby and myself that it is gracious of you to stop by, but *your apology is not good enough for me.* Abby probably, but you showed disrespect for both my wife and me. I am emphasizing my wife, not yours. As you can tell, I have had about enough of the Blake and Abby show. *Why isn't Abby speaking up, Blake thought?*

What exactly does that mean, sir? What is means is that going forward, you are to stay away from my wife, and I mean no phone calls, no lunches, etc. This is where Abby finally spoke up, Colin, I thought we had an understanding that it wasn't necessary to sever all my ties to my friends? I changed my mind on that darling. Why Colin would you do that? Let me be blunt to the both of you, I was not born yesterday, I am not a fool, and I certainly am not a person to fuck with. If Blake were smart, which I can see he is not, he would not have come here so soon or at all if he intended to keep his distance, you, Abby.

They both looked as if Colin was scolding a child. Now there are a few things I want to clear up; one is that Abby has filled me in on your relationships past and present. Next, I think it is time Blake for you to confess to her what really happened in her ex's basement. With that, Blake nearly flew out of his chair and started for the door. Abby stood up and grabbed his arm, "stop Blake, what is he talking about?" Colin escorted Blake back to the sofa then told him to tell the story, or he would. Blake, please tell me, is there something about that day I don't know? Blake gave Abby a look that almost scared her to the core.

Abby, I never wanted you to know this, but I did not shoot Jaci by accident I meant to kill her. Colin saw me, and I must say to this day, he has protected me from being arrested and charged. *Abby was in disbelief; this cannot be true.* Why, Blake, why would you do that? Abby was now crying uncontrollably. Colin handed her his hankie. I thought she was going to kill us! Why would Jaci do that? Earlier that week, she had confessed to me that she wanted to be with me, and she thought I also wanted a relationship. Abby Jaci was jealous of you; she honestly was not a good friend. Colin, why have you never told me? At that time, darling, I thought he was just a friend and not a lover. Had I known what I know today, I would have taken a different path, I can assure you of that.

I am so sorry, Abby, and Colin, I promise this is the last you will see of me. I am a pathetic man in love with a woman he can never have. Rest assured Abby, and I have not been intimate for some time; she has been a friend, but I have made it hard for her to do so. I have tried my best to change her mind over the years to no avail. I need to leave now. I am in intense pain.

Colin walked Blake to the door, "don't worry about what happened in that basement; it's a dead issue, and you did Abby a favor." Thank you! I appreciate that. Good because if you ever see my wife again, I will use that information to have you prosecuted and know this. I do have friends in high places. Mr. Cavanaugh, I have no intention of pissing you off ever again. I'm happy to hear that, Blake. Now go live your life like an honorable man. I think there's one inside you somewhere.

In pain and dragging his ass to the Uber, Blake thought he was lucky to get out of there with a mere warning. That man is a scary dude, but I am more than shocked that he knows about Abby and my affair. I love that woman, but I like living more — time to move on.

Chapter 18

Amanda and Rachel were tossing a coin to see who got the master bedroom. Rachel insisted that she should get it because Amanda would be gone soon after graduation. Amanda, on the other hand, did not agree with that line of thinking. Toss the coin sis, and don't cheat. Fine, here goes, up in the air it went falling unto the carpet. You pick it up, Amanda. I don't want to be accused of cheating. Ha well looks like it's yours, Rachel. As it should be sister. In reality, Amanda never wanted it for the reason Rachel stated. Her plans were to as soon as Colin started the next recruit class. Hopefully, by the end of the summer.

The girls ordered carryout and ate in front of the fireplace. Rachel brought up the wedding reception incident. So Amanda, what is your take on Blake growing some balls? My opinion is, "he has lost his mind." Why do you say that? Going up against Colin seriously, Rachel Blake is an idiot, and I am sure feeling the pain of his stupid act this morning. Well, that we agree on, but you know as well as I do that mom has had a hard-on for Blake since high school. As I have mentioned before, I doubt she has given him up. Gross Rachel, that's a terrible thing to say about mom. Gross, indeed, but I think true.

Abby was out of sorts and kept to herself for the rest of the day. Colin appeared to be disappointed in her behavior, and he told her so. Usually headstrong and determined to have her way with most things, Abby was not used to being outplayed and outmaneuvered. Kudos to her husband, even though she did not like how things ended, she was aroused by his ability to out-smart her. Making plans for a romantic evening, Abby wanted to surprise Colin and let him know how happy she was with the way things ended. *BUNK PURE BUNK!*

Colin was sitting in the sunroom when Abby walked in, dressed in a beautiful black cocktail dress. Darling, you are going out? Yes, I thought I would, but I was hoping you might join me for a romantic dinner at The Chateau. Are you pulling my leg Abby? No way on earth would I do that? Do you want to go or not, Colin? Of course, I do darling you caught me off guard, that's all. Give me a few minutes to get dressed. Wow, so she isn't as mad as I thought.

Colin was pleased and hopeful for his marriage, and the night was off to a stellar start. Dinner was wonderful, now how would the rest of the evening go. Once home, Colin brought into the living room a bottle of wine with two glasses. He waited for Abby thinking she was in the bathroom. When Abby came down the stairs, Colin watched in awe; she had on his favorite negligee. He smiled, thinking about how long ago it was that she wore what he thought was the sexiest thing he ever saw on a woman. Of course, Abby was not only the most sensual woman he ever met but also the most beautiful.

Darling, you look stunning, and you know how much I love that outfit. I do pops I wanted to surprise you do you love it? Of course, I do but not as much as I love you, Abby. I know that Colin and I love you. I was upset earlier, but after I thought things through with a clear mind, I knew you did the right thing. Clearing things up with Blake, I continued seeing him as a friend for years because I felt sorry for Blake. Enough of this, Abby, I don't want to speak of that man ever again. I understand now how about that drink? Colin poured them a glass of wine, and they headed for the bedroom.

Abby sipped her drink while walking to the bedroom; her mind raced with thoughts of how she and Maxim could eliminate Blake once and for all. It had to be done because she knew deep down she could not give him up. Not for anyone. Abby thought killing him would solve many issues. Mainly she did not trust that he would keep his mouth shut about their ongoing affair. But then again, he didn't reveal anything to Colin earlier when he certainly could have. I need to make sure I want to cross this line, other than the obvious that's it's a crime worthy of life behind bars or worse. Of course, I would not do the deed. I would get Maxim involved.

Abby, are you coming to bed? Be right out pops. Colin waited for his wife even though he was not in a playful mood. His feelings for her seem to have changed for the moment. He knew there was more to the Blake and Abby story, but he did want to believe that the affair had stopped. Should he take their word that they had not been in a sexual relationship for at least two years? I know deep in my heart that they lied. Can I ever trust Abby again? I want to for if I don't, she will break my heart.

Waiting and waiting, Colin finally fell asleep. When Abby entered the bedroom, she wasn't at all shocked to see Colin sleeping. Abby had already changed her clothes, so he wasn't aware that she had no intention of having sex with her husband. Earlier this evening, Abby thought it was what she wanted if for no other reason to assure Colin how much she did love him. Who would have known that a special occasion like a wedding could end with so much strife and hurt?

This is all Blake's fault, and I will never forgive him for his actions!

Abby was up and trying to figure out her next step when Colin walked into the kitchen. Abby Lynn, I think we should talk; I have a few things I want to say to you. Okay pops, I agree we do have issues we need to address. But Colin, I don't want to rush into making rash decisions while it's apparent you are upset. Darling, I thought you knew me better than that, "I've never made a rash decision in my life bar one, and that was falling in love with you at first sight." Abby, I admit that for the first time since I met you last night was the first time I found myself without a desire to make love. Of course, I am sure this happens for most couples who find themselves in an argument.

Abby, at this point, felt like the shittiest person in the world. She wanted to say to him how sorry she was and how she also felt the same way. Would those words hurt him even more? Oh hell, jump in there and tell him how you feel.

Pops, last night I also found myself only wanting to keep my distance, I thought putting on that black negligee would entice you to continue to want me and love again. Then I thought, "if all we have is about sex, passion, making love day and night, then we are only physically attracted." But does that mean as the stats dictate that we will fall out of love? Colin saw that her eyes were starting to tear up; he got the box of tissues and handed it to her. Abby, "have you fallen out of love with me?" God no, why would you ask me that? Darling, are you going somewhere with that train of thought then? I'm not sure Colin, but I am scared I don't want us to be like we are at this moment, being in doubt about our love. Abby, it's as simple as this, "do you love me, and do you want to be married to me?" Darling, couples have arguments all the time, this just happens to be our first, and I hope our last. It's such a severe issue, Colin, can you put it behind you, truthfully behind, and keep it there? Yesterday and mostly last night I learned a lot about myself, Abby, a few years ago, I would have walked out on you without blinking an eye. I thought no one is capable of fucking over me and getting by with it. I was a badass, but not anymore. I have changed since meeting you; I would say for the better. The question is, did you actually cheat on me with Blake? My intuitions say yes, you did, but you nor he will ever tell on one another. So I have accepted that it happened.

So my love now the ball is in your court, do you want to stay married, continue to let me love you? Are you saying Colin that you still want me despite what has happened? Even though Blake and I have tried to put your mind at ease by telling you the truth? Yes, Abby, I never want to revisit this discussion ever. It's history, and that is where it will stay, only you or Blake can change our destiny if that never happens then you are I will stay together forever.

Oh pops, I want and need your love, and I very much want to be your wife. We have been through so much; I thrive for some normalcy in our relationship. Well, darling, I can't promise normal, but I can guarantee that I will love you until the day I die.

Colin pulled Abby out of her chair and held her tightly; you can stop crying now love. Let's plan something fun to do today. I even have a suggestion; let's go to the mall and buy that jacuzzi for the patio. Really Colin, then can we go to happy hour at the Bar? If that is what you want to do then its fine with me, now go clean up a bit.

When on a long flight, Maxim found it challenging to sleep. He suffered from "roaming thoughts." Of which he had many, lately, he only thought of one thing or person, and that was Abby. Wishing he had never met her or had made love to her. Never in his life did he meet an unforgettable woman. Knowing she would never be his, he had no choice but to move forward. But when she contacts him periodically all, that managed to do was offer a thread of hope. Hope that possibly she has changed her mind, not a chance, he thought. Abby messaged him because she needs something. And whatever that something is, he knew he would take care of it for her.

Abby, on the way to Washington now, will text when I can arrange to meet, love Max.

Auggie and Diego' put the finishing touches on the graduation program for the recruits. They both could not wait for this class to be over. Auggie texted Colin for confirmation regarding a few loose ends. First, did he approve of their choice for class MVP, Erik Robin, secondly to confirm his availability for the remote access video? Right away, Colin responded with a thumbs up on all issues. Auggie instructed Diego' to set up the equipment and send out the programs to all recruits. This fiasco was almost to an end. Auggie wondered if Colin would change the location of the next class, that is, if there is a future class.

Colin let Abby know the time and place for the graduation and asked her if she wanted to go with him. Explain to me again, Colin, how is this going to work? The graduation is tomorrow; in my office, Joe has everything set up for video conferencing via our computer system. Maybe I will ask Amanda if she wants to join us? I think she would love to do that pops. But you better call her now she's very busy with finals and her graduation plans.

Amanda's phone rang, and to her surprise, it was Colin. "Colin, everything okay?" For once, Amanda, everything is just peachy. Fabulous, what's up? I wanted to invite you to the graduation program for my recruit class, would you be free tomorrow at around five o'clock. Are we going to Costa Rica Colin? Of course not silly, I am doing a remote video program this year. Awe I see, I would love to see that, where should I meet? At my office, do you know where that is? Yes, I took mom there once, should I ask Rachel if she wants to come? Well, if she wants to, why not, I didn't think she would be interested. I'll ask her, but I doubt she will. Thanks for inviting me, Colin. By the way, Amanda, we should have a meeting regarding your plans after you graduate. I want to see if you might want to work in the office here with Joe? Really Colin? I would love too. You see, in a couple of weeks, I will be returning to my corporate office in Chicago. Oh, and how did mom take that news? Abby will be going with me.

Colin emailed Auggie and let him know all the plans for the graduation were in place. Within the email, Colin also added, "Auggie, please find time to research a location for the site of our next recruit class." It should still be in Central America, but this time I want to purchase the property. The area should have an airfield, coastal water access, and jungle-like surroundings. You know the routine and what we need. Keep me informed by email." Oh, don't worry about there being any buildings or housing; I will have those built.

Auggie reading the email to Diego' was delighted they were going to move their location. Diego' smiled and said," thank god." Exactly my thoughts, Diego'. When do we have to vacate this location, Auggie? Not for another month, but I will check with the boss. In the meantime start cleaning up this place, I cannot wait to leave this hell hole. I'm on it, boss!

Colin wanted to speak with Erik about coming to work for Centry Security, but in what capacity he wasn't sure just yet. Colin promised Abby he would step back not only from extended travel but from participating in any role that would put him at harm's way. In his business, being in harm's way was the norm. He could see Erik as a person who he could depend upon for any covert operation. Possibly even a leader. Colin found himself getting excited about returning to work, and his return was way overdue, and for more than one reason. He had already notified his team, and the executive's that he was returning to Chicago soon.

The question was, "would Abby join him?"

Joe and Marty were sitting in their living room, enjoying a glass of wine. Joe expressed concerns about his promotion. Marty smiled and told him. "Joe, you have had extensive training thanks to Colin, and he has faith in your abilities." I know, but what if he gives me an assignment that is out of the office, you know, fieldwork? Colin will not give you any task you are not qualified to do. So stop worrying. Marty, "did I tell you he hired Amanda?" No, but I think I heard a rumor to that effect. I'm happy to have her with me in the office; she's a smart young lady. I think Colin has a plan for her to be an operative in his covert program. What about you, you can do that now that you're a trained professional. No thanks, I'm good inside doing the things Colin doesn't like, accounting, managing his personal life, things Abby doesn't like doing.

Joe, you've never said, "I was wondering if Colin is as rich as I have heard?" Marty, you know I cannot divulge specific amounts. Let me put it this way, Marty; Colin is beyond wealthy, hell I'm not sure even Abby knows his net worth.

Blake thought perhaps he slept through the last day and a half. His entire face hurt; he could barely open his mouth to eat, let alone talk. A sore jaw was a small price to pay for his stupidity, considering what could have happened. He reflected on a past conversation with Abby, told him what she believed Colin was capable of doing if he caught them cheating. At that time, I thought she was melodramatic. Now I know firsthand that he is indeed capable of doing harm whenever he saw fit. Even if he was justified for doing so, they both could have merely walked back to their table instead of attacking me. Well, I was at fault, no doubt about that.

My next step is to wait for my face to mend then focus on my business. Attend therapy at least once a week or more. Join a networking group for singles. Then by the grace of god work on getting Abby out of my system once and for all. Enough is enough, I have been told many times by people close to me that she was a dead end. From my parents to my therapist and some friends. Apart of me thinks she won't give up, I know her well and what Abby wants Abby gets. If she isn't afraid of her husband by now, she never will be. Whether she calls or doesn't, it's of no concern to me; I will not cave into her sorcery. *I can't, I won't!*

Abby noticed Colin organizing things in his office. What ya doing pops? Unpacking and separating personal items from business things. Why? Because I want to move all of the business-related files to Chicago, but I first need Joe to make copies for the office here. I'm afraid to ask Colin, "but why or should I say when are you sending these to Chicago?" Now is as good a time as any to talk about that Abby. I'm listening with bated breath pops. As you well know, darling, I must return to my business; if I don't, I won't have a business. Regardless I want to work, it's what I do, and I have to go to Chicago to attend a meeting and to figure out what my next assignment will be. You're the boss, can't you do that from here? Of course, I can, but Abby, I have a body of executives that depends on my being at these meetings. I might be the owner, but I also answer these people who also have an interest in my business.

So, when are you leaving and how long will you be gone? I am leaving the day after tomorrow, and I will be back in about a week. But Abby, I thought you might go with me. I wanted you to see my house. Make sure it's somewhere you can live a few months out of the year. If I go with you for the week, how much time will you get to spend with me while there? I'm not sure, but I will spend as much time as I can, of course. Darling, you could spend some time shopping and see what if anything we need for the house. What if I don't like the house? Ouch well, it is a lovely home in a very exclusive neighborhood Abby. Let's not worry about that until you see the house. Fine, I'll go with you, but if you can't leave after a week, then I'm returning home. Deal, then it's settled, and I am pleased you decided to go. You know what your motto is, Colin, "any minutes are better than no minutes." Indeed a true statement darling.

Now I need to finish my organizing and get things ready for the graduating class. I need to write a speech, make up a few excuses for such a fucked-up program and decide who, if any, I want to hire to work for me. Would you mind if I went to happy hour? Abby, you don't need my permission to go anywhere, and you know it. I was just asking as a courtesy pops I wasn't looking for your approval. A few of my friends will be there, and don't worry; Blake hardly ever did the happy hour thing. Good grief Abby I am not in the least worrying about that guy, now get the hell out here so I can work.

Abby seemed anxious to see who if anyone would be at the Bar. She was ready with answer's to what she was sure to be a "what the hell was he thinking" session. Sooner or later, it didn't matter to her, it was human nature to question one about a scandal. And this scandal was a doosey. Most of her friend's only speculated about her and Blake, not once did she ever divulge their affair. She was sure Blake did not either. Regardless anyone with a brain could have figured out they were sleeping together.

Two hours had passed, where the hell is Abby? It's seven o'clock, and I am starving. Colin texted her, and to his surprise, she replied. "leaving now, I will pick you up in ten." Abby was weaving back and forth on the roadway; she knew she should not have driven. Lights blaring and blinking I her rearview mirror told her she was in deep shit. Remember, Abby do not take the Breathalyzer test; repeat, do not take the test.

Colin waited and waited for Abby, what the hell is going on. Finally, the doorbell rang; not bothering to use any technology crap; he merely opened the door to find a police officer holding Abby upright. Oh, it's officer Davis what the hell. Mr. Cavanaugh, I have your wife here, and she is quite intoxicated. Officer Davis, please come in and bring her with you, please. It's been a long time; is it protocol to deliver a drunk home? Ha, of course not, but this young lady has been through so much I thought I would do her a favor. For that, I thank you, officer, might I ask where her car might be located? It's about a mile up the road; she was weaving severely when I saw her. This time it's a warning, sir, the next time, if there is one, I will arrest her. I understand, and I am a bit surprised she drove in this condition. It won't happen again, officer, and thanks a lot for the pass. My pleasure everyone deserves a chance, but she gets no more. This is quite the house you built, entire neighborhoods talking about how awesome it is. Thank you, officer, we love it here.

Omg, shit and double shit, Colin tries to get Abby up to bed, but she's like dead weight. He was dreading not putting in an elevator, so many damn steps, I need to get back on an exercise routine and quickly. He puts her on the bed then goes to the bathroom for a wet cloth. Abby, darling, wake up? Colin wipes her face hoping she would wake up. He proceeds to remove her clothes. Well now isn't this situation weird, he slowly had removed everything except her bra and panties. God, this is torture; they had not made love for days. He was about to unfasten her bra when she pulled his face close to her and kissed him. Hi, pops what ya doing? I am trying to undress you, darling. Oh la la, please continue because I am so horny I can't stand it one more minute. Abby, you're drunk! Yes, but not that drunk. Now finish what you started pops. Colin quickly removed her remaining clothes.

He undressed so fast he almost fell over his own feet.

Colin could not figure out how a happy hour led to romantic bliss? Right after making love, Abby quickly went to sleep. Famished, Colin went to the kitchen for some food, not finding much to eat; he thought my god does that woman ever go grocery shopping. He thought not and first thing tomorrow he would go shopping. Colin called Joe and asked if he would take him to retrieve Abby's car. Joe laughed and said, "is there a logical explanation for this situation?" Of course, there is, but you don't want to know. By the way, Joe, are you hungry?

Chapter 19

Joe picked Colin up, and they headed for a late dinner; Joe waited for an explanation, but none came. You're relatively quiet, boss? I am starving, Joe. I haven't eaten food since this morning. That's a long time for a guy your size Colin. What the hell does that mean? It means you are a big guy, tall, big-boned, not small. Are you in a lousy mood Colin? Not a bad mood necessarily just irritated because there is no food in the house, and I need to get my drunken wife's car. Oh, now I get it, Abby went to happy hour and left her car somewhere. If only Joe, it was that simple, yes she went to happy hour but tried to drive home, got picked up by the police; luckily for her it was a cop who knew her, and he gave her a pass. Good god, that was a lucky break boss, does Abby usually drink that much? No, she doesn't, but it has been a stressful few days for us.

Finally, eating and enjoying a beer, Colin felt better. He told Joe about Amanda joining the company after graduation. Joe agreed with Colin in the fact that Amanda was a smart girl and a brave one who would be a good asset. Abby's not on board through Joe, but I think this will grow on her. I wouldn't put that girl in harm's way or, for that matter, anyone who works for me. Excepting, of course, that part of my company that deals with always being in harm's way. Does your company have many employees in the division, Colin? No, I think there are about eight of us, including myself. Oh, I didn't realize you were still active in that area any longer. Well, I am, but only a few people know. Joe, I never want Abby to know I am still active in the black ops part of my business. No worries Colin I don't discuss our business with anyone, even Marty and especially Abby.

Hey boss, I was wondering when you started to plan for your softball team? Joe, lately, that has been the furthest from my mind, but now that you brought it up. I do plan on having a team this spring, why do you want to play? I would love too, and so would Marty. No kidding, that's great. It's a little early, but I think I will send out a group email and see who's interested. Do you realize the team is out of Chicago? No, I didn't know that, but hell, that's not that far. Good, I will let you know the details by email. Now let's get my wife's car before its towed.

Abby woke with a splitting headache, regretting drinking so much. She headed for the kitchen and happily saw the coffee still hot. Where the hell was Colin? Abby went to his office and found him doing paperwork for graduation later that day. Darling, "how are you feeling this morning?" You know perfectly well pops that I feel like shit. Oh, and I wonder why that is? Abby, "do you remember anything from last night?" I know I had a good time, but after I left, I can't remember a thing. Are you aware Abby that you tried to drive home drunk? I remember driving, but I think I passed out or blackout pops, Jesus. I am so sorry. Abby, the police pulled you over, and by the grace of god officer, Davis brought you home instead of arresting you.

I feel so disjointed Colin when I started to drink; I couldn't stop. I've never done that before. Abby, if you think you cannot stress, then you should return to your therapist. I might even suggest you do so before we leave for Chicago next week. Next week that is so soon, Colin. No, Abby, it isn't; if anything, it's way late in returning. Okay, I will start planning for the trip. It's a good thing, Abby, we both need to move on with our usual routines. I know, but at some point, I might want to go back to work, I like my job. That's fine, Abby, but let's talk about that another time.

Auggie had everything set up for the graduation ceremony. He started to see some of the recruits gather in the room, enjoying the appetizers and drinks. Diego' asked Auggie if he was ready to start. Yes, but I am waiting for Colin to login.

Colin, Joe, Abby, and her girls were in their seats, waiting for this ceremony to start. Once Auggie saw Colin's face, he told the recruits to watch the big screen.

Colin speech starts:

Ladies and gentlemen, and I use that term lightly. Laughter all around! I want to thank you for allowing me to address you on this important day via the internet. It is an unusual way and, in fact, the only time I have had to use this method. I will apologize for not being there in person, but as I am sure you are aware, I am still recovering from an injury and not able to fly. So on with the program. First, every recruit has passed to the final testing criteria; you will receive not only the required certificate but also a personal reference from me. You can now pursue whatever field within law enforcement you desire. Graduating from this class has its merits and is held with the highest excellence and respect within the industry.

Now, I look forward to awarding the highest honor to our top graduate Erik Robin, Erik you have surpassed all aspects of the program, you have repeatedly excelled in all of the written and physical requirements of the program. It is my honor to bestow to you the award of Top Recruit of this class.

Congratulations to all, and I look forward to seeing some resumes sent to me for consideration within my company Centry Security International.

And that was the end of the ceremony. Colin noticed Amanda paying attention more so than the others. So, Amanda, what did you think? I thought your speech was perfect and also with a personal touch.

This was the first time Abby witnessed Colin working, even when they first met, she did not attend any meetings he had. Impressive and she saw firsthand how much these recruits respected him. Realizing now that he did indeed need to get back to his business, she felt selfish that she was the reason he wasn't. Oh well, going forward was the path to take because all she wanted to do was forget about the past.

Colin was talking with Auggie when Joe asked if he could leave. No, I want to take everyone out to dinner. Why don't you ask Marty if he wants to join us? Give me a few minutes to finish my conversation. Abby wanted to go home, but the girls wanted to celebrate with Colin; this made Abby happy, especially the fact that Rachel wanted to go. Mom, Amanda, and I have moved some of our things back to the house. That's great Rachel I think you guys will be happy there. We like it, mom, it's better than a college dorm. I imagine it would, but you guys need to keep up with the cleaning. Oh, mom, I'm sure we will.

Nikolai sent Maxim a message and waited for a reply. Even though it has been hell getting approval to enter the United States, he got the go-ahead this afternoon. Nik wanted to get to the bottom of whatever the hell was bothering his friend. Sulking over that woman was a deterrent to his career. Then there is that minor detail of who the hell is he working for. Maxims superior's had only one interest, and that was, "intel regarding any covert operations taking place by the FBI." If Max could not produce, then he would be ordered to return to Russia. That would not end well for Maxim.

Reading Nikolai's text, Maxim was pleased indeed. Seeing his friend while not working was always fun and exciting. But they usually were in a country that offered Russian establishments to frequent. Max knew of a couple of places, but none would be in Washington. I must find a way for us to meet in Chicago or even New York. Max thought he might see if Abby could join them; he wanted Nikolai to meet her, then he would understand my feelings. So Chicago it was.

Maxim sent Abby a secure text, letting her know he would be in Chicago next week, and a friend would be with him. Would it be possible for her to meet?

Abby could not believe her luck; it was fate so therefore meant to be. Even though she would not *unless she had to* sleep with Maxim, she needed his skills to take care of Blake. Of course, he might want something in return, but she would try her best to be good. If only she could trust Blake, killing him would break her heart. If he committed suicide, no one would be surprised. With Colin working while in Chicago, she would have time to meet Maxim. But who is his friend, and why is Maxim with someone?

Colin splurged and treated all to a dinner at The Chateau; he appeared to be in a much better mood. Abby thought this was due to his decision to return to work and his beloved Chicago. She knew it was time and had resolved herself that it was the right time. Their many traumatic events in the last year had kept Colin from physically being available. How can I have so much happiness, along with so much grief? It seems impossible to wrap my head around it all now, but its time for the good times to out weight the bad. If that doesn't happen, then something will need to change. At least when I was with Blake, we had no extreme horrific events to deal with. No special ops, no assassins, no running from bullets.

Once home Abby suggested to Colin that when they returned home from Chicago, she wanted to hire a housekeeper. Hooray and that is a great idea and make sure this person will also grocery shop. Very funny pops, we can handle that by shopping online. We can, but you don't; therefore, we have no food. Oh my gosh, Colin, you are forever hungry. I am, indeed, darling. I'm a growing guy. Well, make sure you don't grow too big. Impossible darling, I always stay in shape and for many reasons, my work, to stay youthful but mainly to attract beautiful young women. Ha-ha pops you have the one and only beautiful woman, and that's me, your wife. Colin smiled and picked up his wife and ran up the steps getting to the top of the stairwell before he almost collapsed. Pops, don't you dare drop me now? This is such a romantic effort. Don't you worry, darling no chance of that happening?

The bed thank god!

Abby Lynn, you are the love of my life. I want you to know that I will never leave you and will do everything in my power to make you happy. Pops, I believe you will. Now shut the hell up.

Blake looked at his face in the mirror with no remorse for his actions. He would do it again, even if no one else could see his motivating reasons, he thought Abby knew. Knowing he was such a laid-back guy, almost a wimp when it came to being bold. All Blake wanted was to show Abby he had some balls. His face and jaw hurt like hell, but the swelling was down, and now his coloring was no longer tan but black and blue.

With a therapy session in the morning, Blake knew he would need to explain what happened to his face. He would lie, of course. What he needed was a private conversation with Abby. Of utmost importance to him was her take on Colin's threats. Did she intend to stop seeing him? After all these years? Why did Abby marry that man? Blake was still in disbelief that she could love any man more than him. If only I had made copies of those journals, then the big guy would see firsthand who she truly loved.

Blake decided to text Abby soon, but he wanted to look more presentable just in case she wanted to meet. Was I setting myself up for disappointment yet again? By the grace of God, why can't I let her go? Am I compulsive and obsessive like she said that night? I'm losing my mind over this fiasco.

Chapter 20

Packed and ready to leave, Abby told Colin she wanted to take her car. He objected mostly because it was too small. Darling, don't you want me to be comfortable? Of course, I do, but I want my car, not yours, it's too big. Well, yours is too small. Okay, you drive yours, and I will drive mine. No, that's not happening, Abby. So then it's my car pops. Fine, you win, I can manage. I don't need a car because I have a corporate limo that picks me up and brings me home every day. Well, La te dah pops.

When Abby and Colin finally arrived at his home in Chicago, Abby was in awe of the size of it, shit she said its bigger than ours. Well, darling, I did try to tell you it was adequate and a lovely home, and you would like my house. You did, and I do. Wow is all I can say pops, I can't believe you didn't try to talk me into living here. You know perfectly well why I didn't, and I knew it was not the time for such a request. I wouldn't have moved here, Colin; the timing isn't right even now. But as soon as Rachel is out on her own, we'll discuss it then. Well, we're here now, so let's make the most of it.

Abby was shocked to see that Colin had a live-in housekeeper. Claire, "meet my wife, Abby Lynn." Nice to meet you miss, if you need anything please let me know, you can reach me by text using this number, she handed Abby a business card. Dang pops, I'm impressed. Why? This is how I lived pre-Abby, darling. I had no idea, Colin. Are you okay with this part of my life Abby, the one part of it that I have kept hidden? What possible reasons could you have for hiding your wealth Colin, I already knew you told me a long time ago. I did to some degree, but while you're here, you will be seeing another side of your husband.

Abby walked closer to Colin and put her arms around him, kissing him passionately. Pops, I'm glad I came with you because I want to know all of you, not just the part that pleases me in my hometown. Now we are on your turf, your hometown, and I am looking forward to seeing you in action. Nothing would make me happier, Abby I've waited for this moment for a long time. I don't think you will be disappointed. Well, so far, I would say I'm a happy woman.

Colin gave Abby a tour of his home, but when they reached the master bedroom, she stood in total amazement. Colin, how many women have you entertained in this room? Oh darling now, you know I am not a kiss and tell kind of guy. Very funny pops but I would like to know. What if I told you I never brought anyone home? I doubt I would believe you. Well, you should because it's true, I wasn't a saint of course, but I did not bring anyone here. Ask Claire, she would know. Oh, I will pops.

As if right on time to leave for dinner, a limo pulls into the massive cobblestone circle. Colin yells for Abby to get moving, or they would be late for their dinner reservation. When she comes down the stairs, Colin still to this day believe how beautiful she was. Abby darling, you look stunning. Thanks pops. Let's get some grub, and I'm starving. Where are we going? Everest, it's a very romantic French restaurant. Is it expensive? Grossly expensive but worth every cent darling. Is this how you usually spent your evenings when you were single? Hell no, I hung out at the local pubs. Do any of them have a good happy hour? I'm sure they do Abby, and we can check them out some other time.

The limo driver held the door for Abby, and then Colin introduced Abby to Edwin. Nice to meet you, Mrs. Cavanaugh. Call me, Abby, please, and it's a pleasure to meet you. It's great to see you home again, sir. Thanks, Edwin; it's great to be here. Well, let's get to dinner before we lose our reservation.

So formal Colin I don't know what to think, all I keep seeing are flashbacks of you in a softball uniform. Oh Abby, how I wish I had one on now, but soon. So you're going to play again this year? Hell, yes, I am, and I already started planning. And that's the Colin I fell in love with, a rough and tough ballplayer. Those days at that tournament are some of the best days of my life pops. I can't wait to follow you around like a sports groupie. Ha, that's hilarious, Abby. Colin noticed Edwin smiling, which was his way of approving his choice in a new wife.

Maxim only had the rental car Jim gave him, but he didn't want to use it for this trip. He wanted no evidence of his trip to Chicago. I need to buy a car; it's a pain in the ass to keep leasing a vehicle. Possibly I can do that before I leave surely; it cannot take that long to pick out a car. I have the cash, so why not. With a google map showing auto dealer locations, he took an Uber ride to the closest one. Already with a model in mind, Maxim arrived with all of his documentation in hand. Showing the salesman, a picture of the car helped immensely, and luckily, they had the same vehicle on the lot, not in a color I typically would like, but Silver was okay.

Driving his new Silver Mercedes sedan, Maxim was ready to meet Abby. Booking a hotel close to Colin's home Maxim thought would make meeting up easier for Abby. He had a few days off, so he wanted to spend as much time with her as possible. Feeling excited but trying to remain realistic, he knew the possibility existed that Abby would not meet in his room. We did have an agreement never to see each other again.

The drive to Chicago was a mere thirty kilometers, and Max was surprised Colin didn't commute this daily. Colin's company headquarters was located so close to Abby's home, but I suppose he had his reasons. In today's technology-oriented world, one didn't need to be physically anywhere. I would not guess Colin to be that kind of owner. No, he had others to do the work for him. The Snowman was a hands-on operative on the outside, not a guy who worked in his office tower.

Maxim thought he knew what Abby wanted, and that would be to rid herself of the man called Blake. I'm okay with that, but the man I want to eliminate from her life is her husband. In reality, that could not happen without the support and a directive from

his superiors back home. I suppose the man could have an accident that could happen to anyone.

Let this thought go, Max, if Abby chooses me over him, then I will make him disappear.

Colin woke Abby up before he left for his office, kissing her then telling her to enjoy her day. Darling, "if you need a ride anywhere, ask Claire to summon Edwin, and he will drive you there." Not necessary pops if I go out which I doubt I will drive, I have a GPS in my car. Okay, well, then I will see you later tonight around dinner time. I instructed Claire to make a special dinner for us. See you later, pops. Abby rang the service bell for Claire and asked her to bring coffee and toast. I could get used to this way of living.

After breakfast, Abby showered and dressed but had not a clue what she wanted to do. Go shopping or have lunch somewhere by herself. She was googling on her phone for ideas when a text came through. Excellent, it's Maxim.

Abby, I'm in Chicago here is the address of my hotel, can we meet soon, love Max? Love Max, ugh that's not good, I need to think precisely how I want to accomplish my mission and how to manage Maxim's needs. I very much would love nothing better than to have a few hours of sexual passion with that man. But I fear he would not let it end in the bedroom. Possibly we could talk it out set some boundaries, who the hell am I kidding assassins don't have rules, let alone any limits.

Maxim, I can meet at the hotel lounge at noon. See you there, Abby.

Noon, Max was surprised she wanted to meet so early, I will make a reservation for lunch. Start natural and relaxed, and we can talk about "the favor." Then I will see if she wants to go back to my room for a drink. I don't want to do anything to upset her until she meets Nikolai. But my heart says, "I want that woman and badly, not only for personal satisfaction but she's bold, intriguing and beautiful. Rarely have I met any female with all of those traits.

Она должна быть у меня! (I must have her!)

Colin arrived at his office and was greeted with much fanfare. Everyone was so happy to see him back in the office. He thought that they knew he was the key to the company's success and sustainability. Managing from a distance was never going to happen again, for any reason. The executive member's meeting was in an hour; Colin met with his assistant and was ready. He knew he could expect backlash for his absence, but none of that was any of their business. They already knew why he was not present for the last three months, so he didn't feel compelled to go over that again. Wanting to move forward merely was his plan for this meeting, no plans to visit the past. If they didn't like it then too frickin bad.

Maxim waited in the lounge for Abby, nervous like a high school boy waiting for his first date. Good god, what the hell is wrong with me. When Abby walked in, he stood up and waved to get her attention. There she is right in front of him, he leaned forward and kissed her not on the cheek but full-on those lips, catching her off guard. Maxim, enough of that sexy greeting. He ignored her and led them to their table in the adjoining restaurant. Abby knew this was not a place Colin would ever visit, so she felt safe. She was anxious more so because Maxim was by far the hottest looking guy she had ever been with. Yes, more so than Blake and Colin together.

God give me strength!

If she and Maxim got caught, she was toast and divorced. Since coming to Chicago and seeing how her husband lived here, she was doing nothing to jeopardize that.

Abby, you wanted to see me and have a talk about a favor you need. I do Max, but why don't we have a nice lunch first. Okay, Abby. By the way, you look magnificent, beautiful as ever. Thanks, compliments will get you far, but I'm sure you know that. I do my love; I have missed you greatly. After lunch, would you please join me in my room for a drink? I thought you would never ask!

What the hell! So much for discipline.

Leave it to Maxim to have a suite, with a sitting area, and a separate bedroom. Abby was glad he didn't get a hotel near downtown. Less chance of getting caught. Once inside the room, Abby could not control herself any longer as she rushed into Maxim's arms. Oh, Maxim, I did not realize how much I missed you. With that, they both started shedding clothes, and before she knew it, they were making mad passionate love. Abby, "we didn't even get the drink we came up here for." They both laughed as he poured them a glass of wine. I'm in an awful mess, Max. What could be so bad that you need me to intervene, Abby? "I want you to kill Blake." Again Abby. "Yes, but this time, we need to make it happen." She then told Max everything that transpired between her, Colin, and Blake.

So it seems like an easy fix Abby, I will make it look like a suicide, he appears to be a candidate for that action. I agree Max, but I care about him, so I do not want him to suffer. I wish my love I was killing your husband and not this weak man Blake? Maxim, I don't ever want you to hurt Colin; you promise me you will not? As much as I would like to see him dead, it is impossible on many levels. The Snowman is a hands-off operative; if I killed him, my superiors would know it was me, and they would not be happy. Who the hell is The Snowman? Your husband Abby, he is a special forces, black ops, and ex-Navy Seal. Don't you know anything about the man you're married too? Apparently not! Ready for round two, my love?

Nikolai landed at the O'Hare airport. He was nervous about being recognized by the security cameras. He was, after all, on the FBI's wanted list by Homeland Security. Even though he was in disguise, it was hard to change much of his face. Fingers crossed as he waited his turn at the customs and immigration entry to the United States. Even though he was ordered here, Nik knew he should not be here. Having close friends, not a good idea in his line of work. He and Max were close and always have been since University in Moscow. Thank goodness he passed through without any fanfare. Now he needed a ride and thought to see if Maxim could pick him up.

Abby caught a cab and decided she should spend some money shopping. Being gone all day without nothing to show for it was not a good idea. A new pair of jeans and a sweater was a good buy. My god, I'm getting spoiled. Last year I would have never spent $600.00 on a pair of jeans. And the sweater cost almost that much it was cashmere and expensive. I might as well throw in a new purse.

Maxim received Nikolai's text for a ride. Shit, he's a day early, thank god Abby was gone. Max texted him back that yes, he could pick him up and would be there in about one half an hour. Maxim got Nikolai a room in the same hotel but not on the same floor. He didn't want him to interfere with Abby's visits. "Was allowing Nik to meet Abby a mistake?" Probably not in the long run, but the purpose was a selfish one. He wanted Nikolai to meet Abby, which would allow him to see why he loved her.

Maxim pulled up to the "passenger pick-up area." Nikolai got in and said, "wow, is this a rental?" Nope, I bought this vehicle this morning. Why? Jesus that should be obvious; I needed a car of my own. I hate to drive that cheap government car. I see it's a nice one, that's for sure, Max. Glad you like it now let's get you checked into your hotel. "Has the woman arrived yet?" Yes, Abby just left we had a wonderful afternoon. How wonderful? Amazingly wonderful, Nik! I hope this affair ends the way you want Max; you are treading on thin ice. She loves me, and I love her, that's all that matters. Well, what should matter is that if her husband finds out you're both dead. Awe, that's not going to happen if I get to him first. Max, I'll forget you said that for now, but you know as I do, "no such thing will transpire."

Claire had dinner ready, and Abby was waiting for Colin to get home. She put on her new clothes, hoping he would comment on how nice she looked. Waiting wasn't one of Abby's good character traits, so she told Claire to serve her and put a plate away for Colin. Surprisingly the food was delicious. After dinner Abby went up to bed to read; maybe she might even finish a book while on this trip.

Colin got home three hours later than he said he would. To say Abby was pissed would be an understatement. Darling, I have no excuse except that the guys wanted to go out for drinks. How wonderful pops, but didn't you think I might want to join you. Sorry Abby, but that didn't enter my mind at that time. It was a guy thing. That's nice, Colin really fucking nice. Leaving me here by myself, which is precisely why I knew coming here would be nothing but annoying. I should just go home. I don't want to be in the way of" business as usual." With that, she got up and went to bed.

Jesus, I can't win with that woman. I should have asked her to join us, but I didn't want too. I promised I would make myself available, and I didn't. This marriage is plaguing me with regrets. I hate that, and I hate myself for being so selfish. What can I do to make amends?

Chapter 21

When Abby ordered her breakfast from the kitchen, Claire brought not only her breakfast but a bouquet from Colin. The card read, "Abby, my love, I am so sorry about yesterday, and it won't happen again; please forgive me. I will have Edwin pick you up at noon for lunch." Please don't say no, let me make it up to you. Love you much, Colin. Well, it's a start, I guess. What an asshole for leaving me here with servants. This is gonna cost him, and I'm insisting Colin take me shopping for some jewelry I have wanted.

Since it's only 8 am, I might see if maxim wants to meet for breakfast. Abby quickly got dressed as she texted Max. "how about breakfast?" Immediately he replied, "where and when?" Now in your hotel room. Maxim was smiling from ear to ear, he alerted Nikolai to meet him and Abby in his room at ten-thirty and not a minute sooner. Nikolai, amused, thought Maxim was indeed in love and was headed for major trouble. He was ordered to step in to stop this nonsense; he had an idea that just might work. It was for Maxim's well being that drastic measures had to be taken.

Abby got her car and took off; she replied to Colin that she not Edwin would pick him up for lunch. No arguments pops we're going shopping after lunch. Colin laughed when he saw Abby's reply, "not shocked, my love. I will buy her whatever she wants."

Maxim waited for Abby like a lovesick puppy; he couldn't wait to hold her in his arms. When she knocked, he opened the door, and to his surprise, standing next to her was Nikolai. Nik, what the hell are you doing here? I thought you said to meet for breakfast. Please come in, both of you. Abby was wondering, "what the hell is this about?" Abby, I want you to meet a friend of mine Nikolai, he is a comrade from my hometown. Abby held out her hand, and Nik held her it and kissed it, along with a not so believable, "so happy to finally meet you, Abby." So this man knows who I am and that's a worry.

Coffee anyone? "Please, Maxim, I would love some," said Nikolai. So Nikolai, are you in the same business as Maxim? Nik looked perplexed and thought about his answer, "yes, yes, I am." "Wonderful, so here I sit with not one but two Russian assassins, how amazing." Nik laughed, and so did Maxim. "What's so funny," Abby asked? Максим, она все, что ты сказала, и она восхитительна. (Maxim, she's everything you said, and she's delightful.) Maxim, what did he say? He said he is pleased to meet you, now have some coffee, Abby. Abby said, "I can only stay a short while Max, but I can stop by later this afternoon for a couple of hours if that is okay with you?" I have a lunch date with Colin. I cannot be late.

When Abby left, Nikolai was smiling, "Max my friend, she is one of the most beautiful women I have ever seen, I can see why you have fallen for her, and she is bold as hell. I almost fell off my chair when she called us assassins." Unbelievable, to say the least, my friend. Now, this is difficult, but you must, and I stress you must stop seeing this woman Maxim. That is why I am here, orders from our superiors. If you do not end this relationship, they have informed me they will take care of this problem themselves. What the fuck does that mean? Read between the lines Max, please, you know they are not messing around. I agree to the point that she is worth whatever one needs to do to keep her, but this is not possible. She's too up close and personal within our business. And to make matters worse, she knows what we do that's just plain crazy.

Позаботьтесь об этой проблеме, если вы не они будут иметь ее устранены. *(Take care of this problem if you do not they will have her eliminated.)* Maxim was in disbelief of this message. He needed to buy some time, so he lied to Nik, "I will end it, but doing so will break my heart." I know my friend, and for that, I am ever so sorry. Let us go to lunch now and drink away our misery, and I do feel your pain.

Я шпион Максим не заставляю меня быть твоим злодеем в этом беспорядке. (I am the spymaster Maxim don't make me be your villain in this mess.)

Abby did not like Maxim's friend, not one bit. She had to hurry, or she would be late picking up, Colin. It was nice of him to plan lunch, but was it enough to take away her anger? Hell no, she's making him take her shopping.

Darling, you're right on time, I have a reservation at a nice quiet place. I think you will like it. Lovely Colin, I'm hungry. It was a small restaurant, but the food was fabulous. "Do you come here often pops?" Not recently darling, but I used to dine here when I was in town. Colin, I was thinking that you might take me shopping for a bit? Shopping wow well, I had not planned that into my day, Abby. I know you didn't, but it won't take long, I know exactly where the shop is, how about it pops can we go? Of course, darling, but I do need to get back soon.

Where are we going, Abby? A jewelry store love, you're going to buy me a present. Oh, am I now, and why would I do that, darling? Because you have been a very naughty man pops. I get it now; this is payback for yesterday. Colin, "you are so perceptive and right on." Abby, "this is not what I had in mind to make up for the errors of my way." Probably not, but its what I want, don't you want to make me happy? Of course, I do, is there something special you have in mind, darling? Yes, I want a diamond ring, a ring for special events, like a cluster of diamonds. Is that all? Yes, that gift will make me happy to be your wife and make amends for your unthoughtful behavior. Good grief, Abby, this going a bit overboard. No, I don't and please do not take lightly how upset I was with you, leaving me with strangers, I did not like it one bit.

Five-thousand dollars later, Abby dropped Colin off at the office. He promised to be home by six. Riding the elevator up to his floor, Colin thought that possibly he was in over his head with Abby. I should have at least called her to say I was running late, but why does she think she needs an excuse to make a purchase?

Abby sends Maxim a text alerting him that she was on her way back. And she added, "hopefully, your friend is gone?" Max was pleased and could not wait to see her, hold her, and make love to Abby. He was frightened that somehow Nikolai might find out, possibly they were watching the hotel. Oh, Max, relax, don't overreact, when I'm ready, I will find a way to see her and keep it secret. Internally his thoughts were.........

No secrets from the FSK Max, and you know that.

Abby knew to be unfaithful to Colin wasn't right, but she could not resist Maxim, he is so exciting and beautiful. Well so is Colin, why can't I be happy with one man?

Famous last words, Abby!

Nikolai was watching incognito within the hotel lobby, and just as he thought, the woman arrived as she said she would. He had Maxim's room wired not only for sound but video as well. Nik prayed that his friend would do the right thing; he hated every moment of this assignment. Love in their line of work is nothing more than a death warrant.

As soon as Abby was inside the room, Max pulled her into his arm's; then they moved to the bedroom as Abby quickly removed her clothes with his help. After an hour of lovemaking, Maxim told Abby he wanted her to go away with him. Max, "you know I cannot do that, not now or ever." Colin would find us and then kill both of us. I doubt he would hurt you, Abby, me well that's possible, but I would kill him first. I don't want to leave my husband, Max. This was not a conversation I was not expecting, leaving with you isn't going to happen please let it go. Abby, "I have been ordered to stop seeing you, by my superiors." "What the hell Maxim does that mean?" It means they said I need to end our affair or else. Or else what? Is that what you want to stop seeing me? Of course not and I won't stop I can't because I love you. I have never loved anyone as I love you, Abby. Panic is starting to take hold of Abby.

That was enough, Nikolai had all the evidence he needed. God, help me! God help Maxim! His team was ready to move, but Nikolai told them to hold back that he would handle this himself. Nikolai knocked on the door but no answer. He knocked again, and then Maxim opened up to see his friend standing there. What are you doing here, Nik? Can I come in? This is not a good time come back later. No, I am afraid not Max move over and let me enter. Max yelled for Abby to get dressed and to hurry. Abby ran for the bathroom with her clothes; she locked the door because this situation did not seem right.

Maxim, "I have seen and heard that you plan to continue your relationship with this woman." Did you wire the room? Yes, we did, and for that, I am sorry, Max, but this has gone on long enough. Now get her out here so we can take care of this situation. No please Nikolai I implore you, please do not hurt her, I will stop seeing her you have my word. It's too late, Max. I have been ordered to eliminate her immediately. Maxim was in disbelief; he could not let this happen, not her, not Abby.

At least let me go to her and say my peace and goodbyes. Then I will leave before you assassinate her Nikolai, but know this Nik, "her husband will hunt us down until he finds us, you do know that, right?" I look forward to the challenge Max, I am not afraid of The Snowman, as you seem to be. You are fooling yourself, Nik, he's a legend, and yes, I do fear the man.

Say your goodbyes while you can; you have five minutes, Max, no more. Maxim goes to the bathroom door and knocks. "What do you want," Abby says? It's me, love, let me in, please? Abby unlocks the door, is he gone? No, he isn't, Abby do precisely as I say. I'm afraid Maxim, what the hell is going on? We are both in jeopardy Abby, Nikolai is here to kill you. This is all my fault, and I am sorry. Kill me, why, Abby was visibly shaking. There's no time Abby, I will fill you in later. I have a weapon hidden under the sink, so I need to get it now, and then I am going back in and kill Nikolai. What, no, I can't be here for that I need to leave. Abby he isn't going to let you leave don't you understand he is here to kill you.

Other than fearing for her own life, Abby thought she might go out there and tell the man she would never see Maxim again. Just let her go, and she would not tell anyone.

Uhm, that's not happened.

Maxim grabbed the gun, hiding it in his sleeve, then he told Abby no matter what happened to stay in the bathroom until he gave her the all-clear. She was too scared to reply. Nodding affirmatively, Max opened the bathroom door. Nikolai asked Max if he would like to leave the room? No, I want to stay, and then he pulled out the gun and wasting no time he shot Nikolai with a direct hit to the forehead. Nikolai fell to the floor, dead. Maxim yelled for Abby to come out. Slowly walking into the room, she saw the man on the floor bleeding, he's dead.

Oh my god, what am I going to do? Crying profusely, Abby had lost it, and that's when Maxim pulled her close to reassure her he would take care of the mess. Take care of it. How? What can you possibly do to fix this, Max? I said not to worry; I have friends here they will help. Abby told him, I need to leave, and now, if I am caught here, I am dead." You're not going anywhere, Abby; you need to stay with me until we clean up this mess. My comrades are on the way as we speak.

Like hell, I'm am not staying here one more minute now get the fuck out of my way.

You cannot leave you are "involved now" I want you, and now I have you, please sit down Abby. What, no way move over Max before I yell for help! That would be a mistake now do as I ask. Maxim, please I have to leave, I need to go home. If I am not back before Colin, he will come looking for me. Not worried, Abby, we will be gone within an hour. Gone, going where? You're crazy; I am not going anywhere with you. Oh, Abby, you have so underestimated my love for you. I killed my best friend and comrade for you; now you think I am letting you leave.

Maxim, I am pleading, please let me leave. Max removes his gun from his belt and aims it at Abby. My love you are not leaving without me, we will go together as soon as my team arrives to clean up. Let's go. Abby is now beyond afraid, and now for the second time, she is being kidnapped.

The "team" arrived and had a conversation with Maxim when they finished he picked up his bag, and they left. Abby, "if you try anything foolish, I will not only kill you but your entire family, nod if you understand." What choice did she have, she nodded that she understood? On the elevator, she asked him if anyone would find the wire. Abby, we are professionals; there will be no evidence that you nor I were ever here.

Hopeful that the elevator or the lobby had cameras, Abby believed Colin would find her, then what? Already thinking of how to explain this debacle, Abby figured she knew the answer.

Lie, Lie, and Lie!

Where are we going, Maxim? Keep walking, Abby. I have a car waiting to take us to the airport.

Chapter 22

Colin arrived home on time, as a matter of fact, he was early. He asked Claire if she knew where Abby was. No, sir, I don't, "she has not been home all day." What the hell, he tried calling her but no answer, he left a message. Another two hours and still not a word. Now he was getting worried. Would she actually come home late just to show him how it feels? No, he thought not. He tried calling her again, and he texted as well.

He called all her friends, and even though he hated doing do so, he called Blake. Without an explanation, he found Blake to be quite helpful and concerned. Colin promised to let him know when she got home.

Something seemed off-center; he could sense danger a mile away. He decided to wait at least two more hours before calling the police.

At ten o'clock Colin calls the police and then Jim.

Jim could not arrive until the next day, but the police were already with Colin. Sir, "we will put out all the stops to find your wife." I'm sure you will officer, but I also will be looking as well, you know who I am, right? Yes, sir, I do, and I am not surprised in the least that you will help find your wife.

Colin was perplexed, where to fucking start. So she didn't come home after lunch, did she continue to shop? He would check their accounts and credit cards first. He called his office and asked for GG, he was a good detective, and Colin knew he could trust Gabriel.

GG arrived an hour later to a boss in much distress. Colin, "I got here as fast as I could what is going on?" First GG, needless to say, this is a private matter, I need your discretion and your help. You have it, sir, as always. Good, here is what I need, get that computer started and check to see if Abby used a check or a credit card this afternoon.

Nothing Colin, she did not use either. Shit, okay, now see if you can ping her car GPS? Already have that going, sir, and the car is parked and not moving. Where is it parked, GG? It's downtown in a hotel parking lot. What the hell was she doing there?

Colin and GG left to see where the Jaguar was parked. GG had his laptop on following the GPS route, and they were getting close to the airport. Jesus, why would Abby be here, surely there is a good reason Colin thought. GG pointed in the direction of a hotel parking garage. And there is Abby's car. GG asked, "you got keys, boss?" Shit GG I don't, I hate that car; it's too small for my body. Any ideas on how to get into it, boss? Of course, I do. I'm going to break into the damn thing. Wait a minute Colin, "what if she's in the hotel?" Hell, I never thought of that GG, but I don't know of any reason she would be here. Maybe she met a friend or something, don't you think we should go in and check it out before we damage that car? Of course, we should.

Colin and GG drive up to the entrance; Colin goes in and asks at the front desk if anyone has seen a woman; he described Abby to them. The one guy says, "do you have a picture?" Yes, I do hold on a minute, Colin gets his phone out and shows them a picture. They both said yes at the same time. When and how long ago did you see her? One of the two guys said, "I worked this afternoon, and I saw her. I would say about one-thirty or so." The other clerk then said, "I came on duty about four, and I think about that time I saw her leaving with a man; she looked strange." Now Colin was confused, why would she be here with a man? And why would she leave her car here? Kid, listen to me, my wife is missing her car is in the garage; this is important. Did it look to you like possibly she was taken against her will? The guy said, "now that you mention it, that's exactly how it looked, she looked to be in distress. But I'm sorry we see all kinds of crap in here."

I need to see the hotel manager now! GG was now with Colin and trying to calm him down. Sir, there is more than likely a logical reason for this. No GG I don't think so, I want to see if they have cameras in this place. Well, sir, I am sure they do.

The manager led them to his office, he called security, and together they searched for any footage that might be helpful. Colin watched as they went from one blank frame to more of the same. Mr. Cavanaugh, this is crazy, but most of the footage is gone like the cameras have been shut-down. Keep looking please if someone has her maybe they forgot a camera or two.

The security guy went from one computer screen to another and then another to no avail. Then he said, let me check the one in the lobby; it's well hidden. I doubt anyone would know where we put the camera. All four of the men were staring at the computer screen when all of a sudden, Colin said, "they're back up a bit, its Abby, and she's with, oh shit, are you kidding me!" GG asked, "Colin, who is that man?" Sir, he looks to have a gun, it's not too visible, but I can see it, can you? The manager now said he was calling the police. Colin agreed and asked if he could get a copy of the film. Of course, give me a minute. Better yet, can you print off that frame?

With a printed copy of Abby and Maxim, Colin told the manager he would come back for a copy of the rest. Where are we going, boss? To the nearest FBI office, GG. But its almost midnight. They don't close; someone will be there because I already called Jim. They know we're coming.

Colin stared at the picture and agreed Maxim did indeed have a gun in Abby's back. What the fuck was she doing here? And with him, this is huge and an international mess.

On their way to the bureau's office, Colin was on the phone with Jim. Colin, this is a cluster fuck, and you know it, what the hell is going on? You're asking me, why don't you keep tabs on your damn assassins, Jim? You know the answer to that, Colin. It's on his phone, but if he's smart, which he is, he got rid of the phone, or it's in Washington. I'm working on that as we speak.

Why Jim would Abby be with Maxim? I have no idea, but you can believe she was tricked or threatened, or she wouldn't have been there. Of course, I think he is retaliating against her because she told you that he was a double agent. Jim, he's going to kill my wife!

Darling, where are you, and what have you done?

ABOUT THE AUTHOR

Lynda L Freeman

The love of anything can come to fruition at any time. Always a writer and an avid reader. My published writing has come at an advanced age (well not that advanced)
All I desire is for readers to enjoy the story, like my character's and keep reading.
I love to travel, am a Disney geek and like being with family and my friends.
For additional information about me and my books please visit my website:
www.lyndafreeman.com

BOOKS BY THIS AUTHOR

The Devil's Music An Abby Lynn Novella #1

Drama, suspense, a love triangle- Abby Lynn is a bad girl. She wants what she wants and intends to keep it. Follow her on a journey for international intrigue, murder and a love triangle so entangled in lust, betrayal and a need to keep her lovers in her life, if only for as long as she wants them in it.

Abby Lynn is a mother, a daughter, and a friend to many, all of whom cherish and love her unconditionally.

Abby likes handsome, intelligent men; she has all the necessary ingredients to attract and keep all she desires.

A career woman in a Midwestern city who gets caught up in meeting the love of her life, oh, wait a minute! Abby already has a lover, is she willing to give him up? Not in a million years.

Follow her quest to keep a balance of loving two men, one of which is very much out of her league. Colin has secrets and a life filled with excitement and some fantastic talents that surface later in their relationship.

Her story is a long one where it ends is yet to be determined; only Abby Lynn can envision her future with not only one but many affairs of the heart involving spies, kidnappers and other various acts of human nature.

The Devil's Dance An Abby Lynn Novella #2

Abby Lynn continues her life with more intrigue and excitement. She is determined to keep what she wants and needs within her reach. Meaning, Colin, and Blake. What is the possibility of an unknown Russian assassin? Abby has entered into her life with Colin without full knowledge of his dark side. Follow Abby on her quest to keep her grasp on reality and beyond.

How exciting and stimulating can managing two lovers be? Abby is a pro at balancing her lover's but at what cost?
Is it possible that Jim has discovered via his investigation that Abby has more than one man? Betraying Colin, his best friend, and professional liaison. What then would Jim do about it?

The Devil's Revenge An Abby Lynn Novella #3

Abby's life has taken a turn for more drama, excitement, and tragedy, but somehow, she always manages to see the glass half full. Colin, Blake, and oh that Russian assassin seem to keep her busy and always on her mostly bad behavior side.
She and Colin experience a personal loss, and it affects their lives immensely. Changes are on the horizon for Colin business-wise.
As a reader of my books, you come to realize that all of this drama can and does happen to a normal, mid-western woman. From the moment they met, the main characters never leave us without providing an open book into their convoluted lives. Will Abby continue to balance the three men close to her, one of which she decided to marry. What the hell was she thinking? Will her daughter Amanda follow in her step-father's shoes? Wanting to become a recruit in Colin's training program for work as an agent of the FBI. Would Abby allow this to happen? And there's Rachel, the daughter who causes her mother much agony because Rachel does not like her husband.
Follow my characters on their journey from lovers to losers.
For suspense along with romance and the many roads these characters take, one must follow them in this series of novellas.